Best wishes
Melanie Myhes

GW00691061

1

Mrs Fisher's Tulip

by

Melanie Hughes

For Mike and Ilona – with love

And for Maddy – who will remember

CHAPTER ONE

I was in a bad mood. It was pouring with rain and freezing, so I couldn't play outside. That always made me cross. And then Julie was coming home and that made me crosser.

Why did they have to make such a fuss of Julie? She didn't even live at home properly, not all the time like the rest of us.

"What on earth are you doing, Sally, staring out of the window like that?" Mum whisked past with a feather duster in one hand and a hoover in the other, like the "White Tornado" on the telly. She always got like this when Julie came home. Barmy.

I decided to concentrate on outside. But the sky was a dull grey and the rain fell straight down like little arrows on the garden I couldn't play in. It was not going to stop. Nor was Mum apparently.

"Come along. All these things out of here now! Julie will be back by teatime and I've still got to make up the bed."

I started to put my games, jigsaws and puzzles into a pile. Julie is my eldest sister. She is an ice skater and she only comes home because you can't ice skate in the summer. For the rest of the year, she goes away. "Touring the capitals of Europe" as Mum calls it. They're a bit soppy about Julie, Mum and Dad. They call her their "firstborn" and everything she does is perfect. Honestly, it's enough to make you sick.

I like Julie in the winter. At Christmas when she's in the ice show in Wembley. She dances on the ice in a pool of coloured light. On her own. I'm quite proud of her then. And she gives me free tickets to take my friends. Otherwise it's much better when she's away and sends me postcards from places with funny names. She's gone for ages.

It's good then because I can have her room. It's the best room in the house. It's huge and it's got a balcony and a dressing room with loads of cupboards and it's own little light. Perfect for secret stores and hiding in. Mum never looks in there. As soon as Julie goes away in September, I get all my stuff together and in we go.

But in the spring she comes back and out I go. And then I have to put up with another sister, who bosses and nags all day long. As if Maggie wasn't enough.

I gathered up all my stuff into a tottering pile so high I couldn't see over it and dropped most of it when I walked into the bed. I was leaving that too. It was a very good bed - perfect for trampolining on and having sleepovers because it's a double so I don't end up with Mel's feet in my face. That tends to happen when we sleep in my bed. Mel is not very big but she's an awful wriggler. She twists and turns all night long. Sometimes she even talks. In her sleep. That's why it's good to have a bit of space between you. In case she goes completely berserk.

Mel is my friend. Best friend actually. We do everything together. I decided to phone her. She could come over right now and comfort me. I wasn't going to suffer like this on my own. She wouldn't want to be left out anyway.

I picked up my stuff again and walked out. "Hell's Bells!" I shouted as I passed Mum. It was the rudest thing I could think of, but I knew she couldn't hear me because she was hoovering the living daylights out of the carpet. Just as well or she'd have been beating the living daylights out of me. For swearing. She'd put a little white rose in a silver vase on the dressing table. Some of its petals had already dropped onto the polished wood. It was all wrong for Julie. Julie is full of life, she laughs and cries a lot. All her colours are more vivid somehow.

8

She always gets noticed first. Why the hell did she have to come home?

Mel said she'd come at once. I knew she would. Because, despite the fact that she can be an awful twerp and we fight all the time, we've been friends since we were two and that counts for something.

Although we both agreed that Julie's return was the absolute pits, at five o'clock that afternoon, we waited, with almost clean hands and brushed hair, peering out of the bedroom window, for the car to arrive. Dad's car. The one that was never in the drive before seven on a weekday. The big black Humber. The one we were NEVER EVER allowed to play in. Dad was picking Julie up from the airport. We loved going there, watching the planes land and take off, seeing all the people coming and going. But Dad had flatly refused to take us, even when Mum asked him. "No, darling." He always called her darling when he wasn't going to do what she wanted. "Out of the question. I'm going straight from the office." And that was that. We never visited his office, not even once. Other kids went to their Dad's offices all the time. Even Mel used to go for at least one day every holiday. But not my Dad. No kids in the office. That was it. It was his "inner sanctum", he said.

"Couldn't care less, really." I was fed up with this whole sister bit already. The fuss, the clean clothes, to say nothing of the room.

" Nor do I. She's not even my sister." Some people had all the luck. Mel only had one sister and she painted all the time so she didn't really count. Imagine the bliss of being an only child.

Mel was sucking her hair ribbon. "Your mother will kill you when she sees that ribbon." I felt like a bit of drama. anything to take the spotlight off Julie.

"I don't care. It's only a school one. Not even best".

That made me fed up. Not only would she get away with it, but she hadn't even bothered to put her best ribbon on. Much as I hated Julie, she was my oldest sister and nearly famous.

And the man in Heggarty's shop, who is a horrible old man who never notices anything, had said that Julie looked like "a film star." She did too. We didn't - Mags and me. Not even a little bit. I was so cross with the whole thing, I kicked the skirting board and little chips of white paint fell off on to the carpet. Mel smirked. "Now whose mother's going to kill someone?"

So I shoved her really hard and she fell over but I had to be horrible to someone, and she cheesed me off with her smug face and only one sister.

The car swung heavily into the drive and we raced downstairs, pushing and shoving to be first and then holding hands to jump the last two steps. We always did that. Mum was already at the door, a proud smile sweeping across her face, her eyes glistening. She had her best pearl earrings on and no apron.

"Oh Julie darling, welcome home." With a clack of high heels and a whiff of perfume my eldest sister flung herself into Mum's arms. We made vomiting noises.

Dad silenced us with a glare as he squeezed past and put Julie's cases down in the hall. They looked heavy. That was a good sign. Presents, you see. Mum and Julie kissed and cooed and took no notice of anyone else.

"Darling, you look wonderful". It was sickening, but true. Julie's dark hair shone, cut and curled, glossy as glass with lacquer. Her lipstick was just the right shade, her skin clear and velvety, and her figure went in and out in all the right places. Julie had glamour, like the magazines.

"She's very sexy, isn't she?" I was whispering to Mel, but she heard me. Her head bobbed up from Mum's shoulder and she winked at me, slowly lowering her carefully mascara'd lashes. Why were hers so long and black? Mine weren't.

"Hello, monster. Whatcha been up to?" She didn't wait for an answer but swept Mum away into the kitchen. Dad followed them.

"I've made your favourite dinner…darling…" The gushing and cooing faded away. Mel wiped her nose with the back of her hand. I sighed.

"Dad's got a new book. It's called "The Longest Day". I think this is it." And we trailed after them into the kitchen.

Then we all had tea - and we had to make our own banana sandwiches while they had a really nice cake with icing and those bright red cherries they put in Aunty Katy's drink. We weren't allowed any. "No cake for you two. It's too late. You won't eat your dinner." It was so unfair - what about theirs? Now dinner, that was going to be a real pill. Mum had been cooking things up for that for days. If anyone had asked me, I'd have rather had the cake and given dinner a miss, but orders were issued and that was it. Sergeant Major Mum. Worse than the army, really.

Julie wasn't too bad. She saw that we were a bit cut up about the cake and, although she didn't argue with Mum, she went straight out into the hall and dragged one of her cases back into the kitchen. Then she opened it right there on the floor and smiled at me.

"Compensation. Evicted you, has she?" So she knew. I thought it was a secret. So I just nodded and looked at Mum. But Julie was rummaging around in the case. Then she pulled out some strange looking packages, like a magician conjuring rabbits out of a hat. They were an awful lot of them. Even a small one for Mel. As sisters go, she really was quite decent.

Then she turned her attention to Mum and Dad. She brought back very odd presents for them - dusty, dark bottles of wine for Dad, slabs of stinky cheese and squashy pate in wax paper for Mum and weird looking tins for no-one in particular. Not a handkerchief or a bath salt in sight. "Confit de canard", "cassoulet", then something called "escargots". Turned out they were snails! Disgusting. Some people will eat anything. Mum crowed with delight when presented with them, but she never actually ate them. She turned them out quietly or gave them

11

away when Julie had gone.

Mags and I knew all about that, but we never said because it would have hurt Julie's feelings. The best things were the fancy foreign dolls and boxes of funny looking sweets she bought for me. They were lovely, always. Mum said Julie shouldn't have spent all that money, but I didn't see why not. I had been evicted, after all.

This time she bought me two dolls. One was a can-can doll, in a pink satin skirt with one leg in the air. She was from Paris and she was fabulous. The other one was a cloth one with thick blond plaits and a straw hat. She was from Germany and not so nice. Then there were boxes of peculiar sweets and little flat tins of fruit lozenges that were shaped like real fruit - baby strawberries and pineapples. They looked gorgeous. Mel and I went upstairs, rattling them in our hands. That was the good bit. But later, after Mel had gone home, there was dinner.

On Julie's first evening home we always had to have dinner in the dining room with the best china and cut glass, and those stiff white napkins Mum only ever used for grand occasions. God help you if you spilled anything on the lace cloth. That had been Grandma's and you'd be joining her in the cemetery if you spilled anything on that.

I hated eating in the dining room. I liked our lovely round table in the kitchen where we normally ate. It was much better because Mum was far less strict in there. It had a nice cosy feel and it didn't matter a bit if you all talked at the same time or reached across someone.

But the dining room was different. Things like manners and elbows were terribly important in there.

"Tell us about your travels, Julie. We want to hear it all," Mum announced adoringly as she ladled out the soup from a china tureen we hardly ever used. I nearly groaned aloud, but Julie had already begun "Well, we had a wonderful evening in Paris before the show opened ..."

Even Maggie was listening with her mouth half open, so

12

you could catch a glint of the metal from the braces on her teeth. She really ought to close her mouth. She looked daft like that. And Maggie was anything but.

"Did you, darling?" Mum said, her eyes soppy with pride. I was beginning to go off Julie. She was showing off now.

"Yes." Julie was getting into her stride now, "We all went - a whole group of us - about ten or twelve or so - to see the Eiffel Tower in the moonlight."

I wondered if I might be sick. That would put an end to it. Julie always talked a bit like that - in that stuck-up, showy way - but she laid it on with a trowel for Mum. Usually Mags brought her down to size. She would let her go on and on and then suddenly wham! She would trip her up and down she'd go! Once she was being really awful, going on and on about how grown-up and glamorous and important her skating friends were and, although we begged her, she absolutely refused to take us to meet them because well, we were "only kids ... and..."

"Just like the audience for your show. What fairy tale is it this year? Babes in the Wood?"

I told you. Maggie was going to be a great surgeon. She could cut off your head with her tongue. And Julie went all red and sort of petered out.

But now even Maggie was ignoring me, staring up at Julie in adoration, the tiny white kid bag she had brought her from Paris on the table beside Maggie's plate. It was very nice. It looked grown up, expensive. Perhaps Mags was hoping some of its glamour would wear off on her. With those braces and her spots she wasn't very big on glamour at the moment, although Mum always went on about her having lovely eyes. I pulled a face at her, but she didn't respond. Now I couldn't even count on Mags. I suddenly felt alone and very tired.

"Sally, wake up! Your hair's in the soup. Sit up straight, child, for God's sake."

Dad was getting annoyed. This dinner was going on forever and we were still only on the soup. But Mum was blind to everything but Julie. She leant forward, her eyes shining,

    "Go on, darling," the worship continued, "Tell us all about Paris."

CHAPTER 2

I went to Mel's the next morning. It was a Saturday. Mum took a tray up to Julie. For breakfast - with a boiled egg and toast and a glass of orange juice. She wasn't even ill. You never got breakfast on a tray in our house. Unless you were dying. We always had to come down to the kitchen and sort out our own cornflakes. Mum was always around and she would sort of supervise, but she wouldn't actually do the whole thing and never ever on a tray.

Mags was already downstairs and shovelling in Rice Crispies. She looked fed up. She rolled her eyes at me when I came in and said, "I should go out today if I were you. I shall. It might be more than you can bear, staying here." Which said it all, really. But I was pleased because the adoring drip of last night had gone and my darling, sarky old Mags was back.

I stood on the stool to reach the cornflakes. I don't like the crisp in Rice Crispies. I like cornflakes when they start to go a bit soggy and Rice Crispies never do, so it's like eating wet gravel, but Mags likes them. I kissed her good morning because I was so pleased with her return to sanity. She wiped the kiss off with her hand, but she smiled at me, so that was all right. "I'm going to the library with Jan. Go to Mel's and don't hurry back." I decided to take her advice.

When I had finished my cornflakes and no toast for me that morning because of Mum being on adoration duty, I went upstairs and got my mac. "Going to Mel's," I announced to no-one in particular as I walked past Mum's bedroom door. I knew she was in there, putting on her lipstick, because I peeped through the crack in the door.

"Sally…wait...", luckily for me, she was halfway along

her bottom lip and couldn't talk properly.

"Can't. It's urgent. An emergency." I declared, sounding as important as I could. Then I raced down the stairs and out of the house before she could stop me.

It was still cold, but the rain had stopped. And I didn't mind the cold because I was free. Out of the house with the whole day ahead.

Spring was coming. The birds were singing and suddenly there were a lot more of them. Thin green buds were all over the trees and the light was that clear white light that Mum said made you notice how dirty and shabby everything looked after the winter. I swung my bag - I always take my handbag, ladies always do, even if there isn't much in it - an empty purse and an old lipstick of Mums – "Fire and Ice" it was called. By Revlon.

I even hummed a song. "Cherry Ripe" which I thought was a good summery sort of song to move things along. I loved summer. I couldn't wait for it. I loved everything about it - the long holidays, sunshine, picnics, butterflies in the garden, ice lollies - everything about it was perfect.

I decided I didn't care about Julie's smelly old room. Soon the whole garden would be mine and I could spend all day long in it. It was my place. Even Dad called the garden "Sally's empire". I think he was teasing, but it was true. From the greenhouse with it's peeling paint and hot peaty smell, to the rockery with the tiny purple and yellow flowers, to the bliss of the pear tree where I could sit for ever and no-one would find me. All mine. No-one loved the garden like me. Mum and Dad talked about it a lot, but they only walked round a bit and then went indoors. They didn't live in it, like me, from the first thing in the morning when the dew made everything sparkle, to the long blue dusk when the shadows grew and turned it into a jungle.

This summer was going to be okay. I could feel it in my bones. That's what Aunty Katy used to say and no-one ever argued with her. Well, it might have killed her because she was incredibly old, a hundred and four or something, and had a face like an alligator and stockings that wrinkled round her ankles. She had been born when Queen Victoria was queen. She had bandages all the way up both legs, like those terrible things in the British Museum that they found at the bottom of a pyramid. Undisturbed for a thousand years. She was quite scary, Aunty Katy.

While I was having a think about Aunty Katy, I met Mrs Braden walking round the circle. She was scary, too, although not as old as Aunty Katy because nobody was.

Mrs Braden had red hair. Well, what was left of it was red and sort of thin and whispy, but most of the time you couldn't see it because it was hidden under her hat. That was truly hideous - it was big and black and she jammed it right down on her forehead so that you could only see these horrible staring eyes peering out from under the brim. It had purple flowers on it on bendy green stalks, so when she walked, they trembled. And she wore a fur stole round her neck, and it was a dead fox, all of it, with the head and paws and eyes. Wide open. I mean I ask you!

She was absolutely frightful and always in a bad mood, but you had to say "Hello" because of good manners. She was Mel's next door neighbour, so if we had been rude, Mel's Mum would have found out. Otherwise I don't think we'd have bothered. Her dog, Secundo was with her, so after I had been polite and said "hello", I leaned down to stroke him, but you had to lean a long way because he was a very peculiar kind of dog. He was a Dachshund and he didn't have any legs. Or very short ones anyway, but he was terribly sweet when you stroked him. I longed to take him for a walk, a real walk, off the leash and let him run in the park and paddle in the stream, but she never allowed anything like that. He had to stay right by her, on this very short lead. And he got grumpy too - just like her - so perhaps it was catching.

Anyway, she didn't say anything to me, which was quite rude of her really, she just let me stroke him and then walked on. And so did I, well, actually I ran the next bit to Mel's because it wasn't far and seeing that poor dog on his leash had reminded me how nice it was to run, so I thought I should really for both of us.

Mel was waiting for me. She was swinging on the gate in the front garden. It was a very good kind of gate because there were two of them, so we could both swing at once.

You aren't supposed to swing on gates. It's bad for them. But we always did, so I got on the other one and started my swing, telling Mel how dreadful things were at home, what with the adoration of Julie and everything.

It made me feel much better. And then we went indoors for a play. Mel had this aunt called Peggy, who Dad said was "a bit of a girl". I wasn't sure what that meant, but Mum shut him up and looked cross, so it couldn't be good. Which was odd, because she was very nice. She let us dress up and play in the garden in her evening dresses and wear her jewellery, which was lovely and sparkly and she had a lot of it, so you could wear everything at once if you were going all out for glamour.

And we did because our mothers would have killed us if we had worn their evening dresses AT ALL, let alone in the garden, but Peggy just laughed and put a dab of her scent behind our ears. It was an awful stink, but it was very nice of her to share. It came in a pretty green and white stripped box and was called "Ma Griffe" by Carven. Mum always washed it off.

So we had a great play, in Mel's room this time because it was still a bit cold for the garden, and we played queens and princesses. Mel likes history, but I think all those kings and queens are a bit much because all they ever did was kill each other, so after a while, we played Snakes and Ladders, which was much more exciting.

Then we got out of the ball wear and went down to lunch. It was Saturday and only sandwiches because Mel's Mum

18

wanted to go out shopping, but she cut up the ham sandwiches into little triangles and stars, which was a bit babyish but still nice, and you got slices of cucumber and tomato with it and a bag of crisps with a blue paper twist of salt. She said she was sorry it was all in a rush and I told her not to worry because it was a big improvement on breakfast. She smiled then and asked if Julie had come back. So I told her all about it, the adoration and the awful dinner, everything. She was the kind of person you could tell things to, she just listened and didn't interrupt, and then she said she expected Mum wanted to make a fuss because she saw so little of Julie if you took the whole year into account, and that she was sure things would settle down soon. Then she gave us both a Kit Kat and an apple.

We went out into the garden then for a private talk, but we didn't stay long because we were beaten back by the cold. So we played Scott of the Antarctic in an igloo on the ice under the dining room table. That was a very good game. We went out into the snow to find the help which never came and then we crawled back into the igloo to die. We suffered horribly. It was a lovely afternoon.

When I walked home at teatime I felt much better and a bit sorry for Mum because it must have been quite difficult to cram all Julie's mothering into six months instead of spreading it out across the whole year like she could with Mags and me. And Mel's Dad said that we had been so quiet while he was watching his football on TV that he gave us both sixpence! So it really was the perfect day and I was going to spend it ALL in the sweetshop on the way home.

I walked home very slowly, to put off the awful moment when I would have to face more of the adoration, so I went the long way round, to drag it out and also because it took me past the sweetshop.

It was a very small shop. More like a big cupboard really because one step inside the door and you were right up against the counter. It was heaven. Rows and rows of sweets spread out before you in small compartments, with shelves of tall glass jars full of sweets of every colour, reaching all the way up to the ceiling. Mrs Turner, who owned it, had to climb up steps if you wanted any of them.

The sweets I liked best didn't come in packets. They were better because you could see exactly what you were getting and how much. All my favourites were there. Gobstoppers and bright pink ha' penny chews shaped like fish and seahorses. I liked the seahorses best. Flying saucers and sherbert fountains, liquorice laces and allsorts, red and yellow pear drops and chocolate covered nuts and raisins. And behind all that in coloured paper wrappers were the chocolate bars - Frys and Cadburys and that funny shaped Toblerone that you only got at Christmas. It was more for grown-ups really, because it was very hard and could crack your teeth if you weren't careful. Like sugared almonds, which looked so nice in all those beautiful pale pinks and blues, but when you bit them, they shattered and it was like eating splinters. You had to watch out for those. They were the sort of thing Aunty Katy gave you for Christmas.

I said " Hello" to Mrs Turner, who came out from the back of the shop when the bell thing on the door rang and then I started to choose. I took ages. You had to think carefully because if you got it right you could get an awful lot for sixpence. The chews were only a ha'penny each, so you could get two dear little seahorses for a penny. I chose some and then changed my mind, but Mrs Turner didn't mind. She was used to us.

I thought again and made my final choice: two seahorses, a liquorice lace, some pear drops, a couple of flying saucers and some chocolate buttons. They were better than the caramels, which looked nice but made you feel sick.

Mrs Turner counted them out for me and put them in a paper bag. I was quite sad to hand over my lovely sixpence, all silver and shiny, but I was very pleased when I felt how heavy the bag was.

I said goodbye and thank you and then went outside, weighing the bag in my hand. After a bit of a think, I decided I deserved a flying saucer what with all the fuss going on at home. So I put it on my tongue and waited for the sticky rice paper to dissolve, and then shuddered a bit when the sharp, lemony fizz of the sherbert kicked in. It was very good.

I walked along slowly, concentrating on my sweet. And then I saw them. Julie and David Thingy.

They were just standing there, staring at each other. The way your mother told you not to. As if they were all alone somewhere - but they weren't. They were standing in the middle of a crowded street at teatime. I waved, but they didn't notice. I might as well have been invisible.

What was going on? Julie had known him for ages. I think they were at school together, but that was before my time. I didn't notice boys then. Now he wore a shiny black jacket with a very thin tie and pointy shoes. His hair was different too, it was all slicked up into a big lump that hung over his forehead. He had his hands in his pockets and was leaning over Julie, standing far too close. He looked a bit daft.

Then he saw me. "That's your little sister, isn't it?" Julie turned her eyes slowly away from him as if she were unglueing them.

"Yes." She didn't look very pleased to see me.

"Hello, Julie." I tried to sound a bit cheery. I mean, one of us had to keep up appearances.

She sighed. A big, dreamy sigh that made her bosoms go up and down. She had good bosoms. They stuck out and she always wore things that showed you they were a nice shape. Men looked at them a lot, so you could tell they were good. I was hoping they ran in the family.

"Didn't I buy you enough sweets from France?" Oh Gawd Luvaduck. That was what Mrs Braid, our charlady, always said when she came a cropper. Like when she smashed the family vase Aunty Katy gave Mum for Christmas. Mrs Braid

21

was super, she played cards with us when she had time and always took a swig from Dad's whisky. For medicinal purposes only, she said. She had a cigarette that stuck to her bottom lip no matter how much she talked. It never fell off. She was fabulous. Woodbines they were called. She usually kept one behind her ear for later.

Julie was glaring at me with her pink, shimmery mouth in a hard, tight line. I waited for the axe to fall. Perhaps she was going to tell Mum. That meant big trouble - sweets before tea were not allowed. But David Thingy just laughed and said, "Come on, Julie, have a heart. Can't have too many sweets at her age. Got any peardrops, kid?"

She laughed then, which she wouldn't have done if we'd been alone. So I had to give them one. Each. Which was a bit of a blow because I only had six. Four now, but he had sort of rescued me, so perhaps he wasn't too bad. We walked home together. But when I got to the back door, they were still standing by the gate. Not talking or laughing - just staring at each other.

CHAPTER 3

She didn't tell Mum about the sweets. And after that things did settle down, just as Mel's Mum had said they would. Mum must have got most of her adoring done during the day when we were at school because the evenings calmed down, and we went back to having supper in the kitchen, with elbows and reaching across each other for the tomato ketchup. We sort of reverted back to our two camps - Mum and Dad talked mainly to each other about what kind of day they'd had and Mags and I moaned on about the awfulness of school. Julie was a bit out of it. She didn't seem to fit in to either camp, really. And now she'd told everyone her stories, she was rather quiet. Dreamy almost.

About a week after she came home, she went to see Mr Heggarty about getting her old job back. She always did that. She'd worked for Heggarty's ever since she left school and he kept her old job open for her when she wasn't on ice. Dad said it was very kind of him, but I didn't think Mr Heggarty was kind. He was a horrible, grumpy old man with bad breath and hair in his nose and yellow teeth. He looked rather like a dog except he couldn't run and jump and catch a ball. He stayed in his shop in an old grey overall and shouted at people instead. It was a very peculiar shop. The shop window was full of hifis and radiograms set out like a little room with an armchair and an empty bookcase and a pot plant, and then when you went into the shop, it was very dark and you had to walk through rows of gleaming white refrigerators and washing machines and spin dryers, all lined up like teeth. It was awful really, like walking through a huge, metal grin. Then at the back the lights became very bright because there was the record counter! And in the summer behind the counter on a high stool sat Julie. She sold a lot of records. Her friends came in to chat and hear all the latest stuff and Mel and I sat about for as long as we dared after school because it was cool, you see, hanging about in a record shop, even if you were in school uniform.

On Saturdays a lot of men came in and listened to things like Oklahoma and South Pacific because they went on forever. But Mel and I weren't fooled. We knew they came in for a look at the bosoms, and I think Julie did too because she gave them short shrift. I mean she played their records because she had to, but when they started the smarm routine she would turn away and pretend not to hear. In the end they had to buy a record just to get her to talk to them. One man bought four copies of Showboat in three weeks. He must have been desperate.

In the winter Mrs Heggarty took over from Julie and they didn't sell nearly so many records. She was old. No-one wanted to look at her bosoms. So the winter was a dead loss in the record department. That's what Mr Heggarty told Julie, anyway. I overheard him when I was supposed to be listening to Bobby Darin.

Anyway, with Julie at work now every day until six, we had Mum back. She resumed the normal Mum stuff - she started making my toast again and checking if I had money for the bus and no more trays, but she also started nagging about homework and clean socks and not leaving the towel on the bathroom floor, so she was a bit of a mixed blessing.

I was beginning to think that a working mother, like Mel's, would be a good thing. Well, she wouldn't be on patrol all the time and it would keep her out of our hair. Perhaps she could go the office with Dad.

But then one day everything went wrong at school. I failed the spelling test and Miss Woodhouse shouted at me, then I had a row with Mel and fell over in the playground. I came home alone, crying. Mum stopped her ironing and asked me what was wrong, so I told her. She asked me if I was too old for a cuddle and I said no, not today I wasn't. So she gave me a really good one and then I sat at the table and told her everything while she made cup cakes with pink icing because they're my favourite. So she was all right really, even if she was a bit silly about Julie.

It was getting warmer now and the days were longer. The garden was becoming possible again.

* * * * * *

The next day after school it wasn't raining, so I went out into the garden after tea. To begin taking stock after the winter. I climbed to the top of the rockery and looked out across the garden. The rockery was my boat, you see, full of tiny flowers and hidden treasures, and in it I sailed across the broad sweep of the garden sea. In it I could be Scott of the Antarctic or Captain Cook with a hold full of peculiar plants no-one had ever seen before. I could perish, founder on lonely shores or discover an island paradise or a new world. Nobody bothered me - no-one spoiled my game. Ever.

I could go anywhere and be anything. I sat down on the broad flat rock that was at the very top and hugged my knees. It was still a bit chilly and the stone felt damp. But it was good to be back, to have it be all mine again. I loved it to die.

"Got any pear drops, kid?" He startled me so much I nearly fell off the rock.

I was furious. How dare he break all the rules and disturb me here? He was standing on the pavement right by the low stone wall. He kept smiling with his silly, creamy smile. I hated him. He had ruined everything. I scowled at him.

"No. You and Julie ate them all." Which wasn't true but he'd get the message. I turned my back on him to make sure that he did. He could keep all his smarm for Julie. I wasn't having any.

"Oh. Sorry." He sounded as if he actually was. I turned round.

"Look, sweetie, is your sister here?" He was almost pleading.

"Which one? I've got two." I hung on to my scowl.

Then he laughed. "Julie, silly." Somehow I didn't mind that he'd laughed and called me silly. It wasn't a mean laugh at all, it just sounded as if he was happy to say her name.

"She's out." She was still at work actually, but I wasn't going to tell him everything, what with him having spoiled my game. But now he was smiling again and climbing over the wall! He had a nerve. And he didn't look at bit bothered - as if marching into other people's gardens was something he did all the time.

"Get back or I'll call a policeman." Mum had told me to say that if I felt someone was bothering me.

"Don't be daft. You wouldn't, Sall, would you? We're sort of friends."

I hated being called Sall. But he was standing at the bottom of the rockery and being so nice, and even if he did have twerpy hair and witches shoes, he was almost grown up and none of my friends had a grown up boy who would even speak to them.

"Look, Sall, I need you to do something for me. I wouldn't ask if it wasn't really important." And he fished about in his pocket and brought out a crumpled Crunchie bar. He handed it over to me. I didn't really like Crunchies, but I took it anyway, because I could always swop and it would have been rude not to take it, after he had said we were friends.

"Okay." I didn't really want to help him at all, but I found myself doing it. It was very odd. It was a bit like taking a dog for a walk on a lead and finding out that it was actually dragging you along and suddenly you had no choice at all where

26

you were going.

"Tell Julie I'll wait for her behind the practice wall tonight - after work." We lived in a private road, just off the tennis club, which we all belonged to and which had the most enormous grounds. Perfect for ambush. You could roam around in them for hours and never see anyone.

"Please tell her, Sall. Tell her I've got to see her. It's really important. She'll understand."

I nodded again. And with that he was clambering back over the garden wall with his long, spindly legs as if he were a bit ashamed. Or in a terrific hurry. He was weird. But somehow, I liked him. And he had said we were friends and made an effort with the Crunchie bar. It wasn't his fault I didn't like them. So I waited for Julie to come home and when she did, I dragged her into the downstairs loo with her coat still on and I told her. She went all pink and hugged me so tight I could hardly breathe. I decided to keep away from those two in the future. They were nuts.

She did meet him that night because she came back late for supper. Late with her hair all mussed up and her lipstick gone. And when Dad asked her why she was so late because we had nearly finished our mains and were dying to get on with the pudd (which was apple crumble and my favourite), she said she'd had to post a letter. Which was a lie.

* * * * * *

There was a lot of lying after that. It started off with just one or two and then it sort of built up and for a long time, I couldn't understand why.

She saw David all the time. I mean, all the time they weren't both at work. Always in the evening after work and sometimes early in the mornings, but never for very long. I knew because I saw them. Well, their secret places were mine, too. The grounds of the tennis club, or the woody bit behind the stream in the park - the sort of places where you could be alone and no-one would find you unless you wanted them to. But they never went to the pictures or for a Chinese meal or a drink in the pub - the sort of things normal people do when they're dating. I mean, they did all the dating stuff, like holding hands and staring at each other looking soppy, but they didn't actually do the dates. It was very odd.

But I didn't let it worry me because they were bonkers anyway, and summer was coming on and I had more important things to think about. Like could I finally swim on my own without that awful rubber ring, which made me look like a baby, but I tended to sink without?

And the school play - I was the Third Gypsy with a tambourine with ribbons on and a swirly skirt, and we sang a song and did a little dance - except Elizabeth Earle couldn't tell left from right and kept crashing into me.

So I forgot about Julie and David, except when she lied to Mum about where she was. All that rubbish about Julie being kept late at work when Mel and I had walked past Heggartys hours before and it was all closed up and the lights out. I couldn't understand why she had to lie and it bothered me. Because she never told Mum the truth. Not once. Now, I understand why you have to lie if the axe will fall when you don't. But Julie lived away from us for six months of the year and she was nineteen years old and had her own money. She had a job and she could do what she liked. She didn't have to ask for permission or anything like we did. And Mum knew she had boyfriends because she'd had them for years.

Ever since she was at school. Dad said there was always "some besotted boy sniffing around after Julie" and he was right. It was because of the bosoms. In any case, whatever Julie did - roasting babies or stoning small birds - would have been just fine with Mum because Julie was perfect. In her eyes. So why did she do it?

I asked her once. We were alone together on her afternoon off, sitting at the kitchen table. Mum had taken Mags into Harrow to buy her a new geometry set (Imagine needing two! One was going to last me for life, I had decided). Julie was doing her nails, painting them a lovely pearly orangey colour, Tangerine Dream by Revlon, it was called, and I was painting a tree for Art. It wasn't going very well - this tree - the leaves were too bunched up so it looked like broccoli and the paint had run, so instead of a nice dark brown for the bark and bright green for the leaves, it all went a horrible kind of khaki. I hadn't known what that was until Mags had leaned over my shoulder on her way out and said, "Oh! A khaki tree! How original. Is it camouflage or Modern Art?" She could be very sarcastic, at times, Maggie. A bit rotten, actually.

I didn't know what she was talking about until Julie told me. And then I was a bit fed up, so I decided to abandon the tree and concentrate on something more promising.

Julie looked like a better bet, more colourful anyway, because now her fingernails were all done, shining and bright, and she had waved them about a bit to dry, she started on her toenails. She propped her bare feet up on the table. Mum would have killed her.

"Julie ..." I knew I had to start gently so she didn't tell me to buzz off.

"Yeah ..." She was frowning because she had overlapped a bit and painted her skin as well as her toenail. She wiped it off quick before it could dry. "What?"

She wasn't being very helpful with this conversation, so it was all up to me.

"You know you and David ..." She smiled a silly, secret smile.

"Why don't you ever do normal things?"

"What do you mean?"

"You know, like everybody else on a date."

29

"We do. Anyway," she started on the next toe, "Shut up. You're just a child, Sally. You don't know what you're talking about."

That made me cross. "Yes, I do. Why doesn't he ever take you to the pictures or for a Chinese?"

I was getting quite worked up now. I think I got a bit carried away on her behalf. She was my sister, after all.

"Why can't he ever take you out like everyone else? I mean, you look all right and he can't be broke 'cos he's got a job. And it's not as if you smell, like Katy Fisher. You've got lovely clothes and you're a skater - you skate on your own sometimes and your name's in the programme, so he can't be ashamed of you. I mean, with all that, you shouldn't have less than everyone else."

She was staring at me now, saying nothing. I went on. "He really ought," and I said this with great emphasis because this was what Mum said when she was complaining about Dad, "he really ought to treat you because you're the lady."

If she didn't understand that, we were sunk. But she smiled - a funny, crooked smile that looked as if her mouth hurt. "Oh, Sally, you are sweet ..." Good, she'd got it. I didn't let her go on. "Do you want me to tell him for you?" I told you, I was completely carried away by this sister thing.

"God, no. It's not his fault, Sall. Things are just a bit difficult at the moment. He buys me all sorts of things."

Well, that was an angle I hadn't thought of. But I didn't want to be fobbed off so I took a hard line. "Like what?"

"Look." She heaved her big squashy bag onto the table and tipped out all this stuff. A tiny teddy bear with a tartan scarf because David was a Scot and his name was MacSomething. Thank God he didn't wear a skirt. They would have looked a right pair of idiots. Then there was a key ring with a silver heart - "real silver" she said, stroking it. And that was it. The rest was just a load of old junk - a dead flower he had picked her from someone else's garden, a dollar bill torn in half, he had the other

30

half she said, as if it was something clever, and a squashed up bar of her favourite chocolate, Fry's Turkish Delight. She didn't want to eat it because he had given it to her, she said. I hoped she would give it to me because even though it was all bashed up, I quite like Fry's Turkish Delight, but she didn't. She put it back in her bag.

"There, see." I didn't, actually, "see" at all. I knew about Diamonds being a Girl's Best Friend and this was all a bit dismal. Rather like him.

She must have twigged because she went on. "And he bought me a record." Big deal. She could get all the records she wanted herself because she got them cost from Mr Heggerty. She had records coming out of her ears. There were so many they were all piled up on the floor in Mags' room. Next to her horrible model of a skeleton with all his muscles on. You didn't want to bump into him in the dark, I can tell you.

I must have looked unconvinced because she decided to come clean. "He's lovely, Sall, and he really loves me. He always has. It's just that things are a bit difficult right now. It has to be a secret." I didn't see why.

"You can tell me. I'm your sister. I won't tell anyone, I promise. Not even Mel." I couldn't see how that would work, but if she needed me, I was prepared to go all out for her. She laughed.

"Oh, Sally, you couldn't keep a secret for two minutes. You'd get in a miff or Mum would crank up the pressure and you'd crack. You always do." She had a point. Mum must have been trained by the Gestapo. She could crank up the pressure something rotten.

"Look, you'll just have to wait a bit. I can't tell you, sweetie, really, I can't. It's not my secret to tell. It would be a terrible betrayal of David." I didn't see why. She'd only just started seeing him again last week. Before that she hadn't seen him for ages.

"But, in the meantime, and because you really are a

darling old goose… I'll do your nails, if you like."

Like? I was in heaven!

"But you won't tell anyone, will you? Promise? Cross your heart?"

I nodded. So that's how I got ten glowing orange nails. I mean, you could practically see them in the dark! Now I had glamour. Soon I would have hair lacquer and lipstick and the most wonderful bosoms like Julie and a much better boyfriend than silly old David Thingy. She even let me wear her stilettos too. I wore them all around the kitchen and practised being glamorous. It was bliss. Then Mum came home. She went bananas about the nails and ordered me to get it ALL OFF RIGHT NOW! I told you she was trained by the Gestapo. She could be an awful old Tartar at times.

* * * * * *

So I never did find out why Julie lied. Not then. Not until much later and by then, it was really too late. I don't suppose I could have done anything about it anyway. Nobody ever listened to me.

But, from then on - after the nails, I was firmly in Julie's camp. We had a secret. She said it was our secret and I liked that. Knowing things other people didn't. Being the only one who did. It made me feel important.

David wasn't my idea of a dreamboat, but she really loved him. And for a while he made her happy. Happier than I had ever seen her before.

She sang in the bath and winked at me in the mirror when we cleaned our teeth and raced out of the house really early, all glammed up. She - the breakfast on a tray, never get out of bed before noon- girl! She was the first downstairs now. Even before Dad. She hardly ever yelled anymore. She even took to doing my toast to help Mum, but it helped me too because, like me, she was a firm believer in strawberry jam. There was no "sugar isn't good for you" business with Julie She piled it on our toast and we ate it together.

Maggie felt a bit left out, I think, but she didn't say anything. Julie was pretty nice to her too. She used to wash her hair and curl it for her. That was an improvement, but it didn't last long because Maggie's hair got greasy and the curl would sort of droop. Dad said that Julie was a joy to have around these days, and, in a way, she was. Her happiness sort of rubbed off on us. He said it was because she had grown up, but I knew different. I smiled when he said that. Because grown ups are the most miserable, bad tempered bunch of people in the universe. Everyone knows that. Except them. And we laughed at them sometimes, because you couldn't help it, they were so smug and so wrong.

She looked wonderful, too. More wonderful, if that was possible. That summer she had a blue and red dress with a swirly skirt and a tight belt and red high heeled sandals with no backs. In the mornings, she used to run out of the house to meet David, her heels clacking, her secret smile in place, and she walked down the street as if she were flying. She was on another planet, but it looked like a very good one. And, as Mum started shouting at Mags and me to hurry up and not forget our satchels and tennis rackets and what about dinner money, I wished I were on it too. Because they made each other happy and nothing else really mattered. I wished I could have a man of my own to love, even if he was a twerp. Someone to make the awfulness of Miss Riley and spelling tests disappear. I didn't know if he loved her - I couldn't tell, but I did know that she loved him. It shone out of her like light. While we struggled into our blazers and panama hats with elastic under the chin, she swanned past us all, out into the new, shining morning to meet David behind the club house. It did seem unfair. Although, looking the way we

33

did that summer, Mags and I, perhaps it was just as well we didn't know any boys. We'd probably have scared them to death.

CHAPTER 4

It wasn't long before Mel found out. She should have been called Sherlock. You couldn't hide anything from her. She was like a bloodhound.

It was after school. We'd been playing in the yard outside the backdoor. I had a pogo stick, well, actually I had two. They weren't really mine, I had inherited them from my sisters and it wasn't going very well. I couldn't get the hang of it. I could pogo all right, but once I started I couldn't stop, so I always ended up crashing into a wall or getting tangled up in the washing line. Mel wasn't much better. Maggie even stopped doing her homework to watch us from the kitchen window and she was laughing her head off. So we decided to retire to the circle where we could either miraculously improve or fail miserably in private.

That was what we thought. What we had forgotten was that it was a Wednesday. Wednesday was Heggarty's early closing day.

It was a lovely afternoon. Spring looked as if it was turning into summer at last. The trees were covered in blossom. The sun shone and it was really warm. We had to take our cardigans off. That was another reason for pogo-ing on the grass. It hurt less when you fell on it.

We chose a lovely long stretch of grass by the side of the clubhouse and we were even having a bit of a race. Mel was ahead, but only by a little, when she stopped all of a sudden and fell off. I thought the silly goat hadn't seen the dip in the ground, but then I heard the yelling.

"For Christ's sake!" It was Julie, hair on end and all red-faced, sitting up crossly and pulling down her skirt. For a minute you could see her suspenders. "What the hell are you doing here?" She was really yelling and Mel looked appalled. Mel has very pale skin and when she's scared it goes sort of paper white. Now she looked as if she might drop dead. How would I ever explain that to her mother? Mel wasn't used to this sort of carry on. They didn't scream their heads off in her family. I had to rescue her. So I fell off my pogo stick and raced towards them, yelling "Leave her alone".

When I got there I saw that Julie wasn't alone. David Thingy was lying beside her in the grass. He was laughing. Then he stood up and tucked his shirt into his trousers.

"Not you too! It's the peardrop kid. Pops up everywhere." He was still laughing. He didn't sound at all cross. But then we hadn't seen his underwear. I turned to Mel. She looked awful. Her mouth was open.

"You can laugh. You've murdered Mel. Look at her. You'll go to prison, mark my words. Both of you." I put my arm around her. Someone had to look after her.

Julie looked across at Mel to assess the damage. Then she sighed. "God, Sally, you do pick your moments." She was such a cow. She'd killed Mel and all she cared about was her stupid secret. I lost my temper.

"You're a selfish fat cow." It was the worst thing I could think of. "How is it my fault if you lie around in the grass terrifying people ?"

Then Mel piped up. "We only came to pogo. We didn't know you were hiding in the grass." She looked as if she was going to cry. She was such a twerp. They fell about laughing. I glared at them and picked up our pogo sticks. Julie came over to us and put her hand on Mel's shoulder.

"Look, Mel, don't be upset. It's not your fault." Then she turned to me, "As for you, Sally Palmer, you're supposed to be keeping this secret, not bringing people along to watch." She was still cross with me. "And I'm not fat. For your information."

I knew that would get her. I tried to whistle to show I wasn't sorry, but all I managed was a sort of breathy fart. David was in stitches now. Julie kicked a tuft of grass as if she wished it were me.

David recovered first. "Look, the only thing that matters here," he really did sound quite grown-up sometimes, "is that you don't tell anyone. Either of you. Because if you do …" here he looked really worried, A well, people other than us could get hurt. You do see, don't you?" We didn't, actually, not at all, but we weren't sneaks. Telling was serious, we knew that and we didn't do it. We had standards. I told him as much.

"Great. You're a good kid, really." He sounded awfully relieved.

"A good kid! She just called me a fat cow!" Julie didn't care about selfish but she wasn't going to forget fat in a hurry.

"Oh, come on, Julie. That was only because she was worried about Mel." He was a peacemaker, all right. Perhaps he worked for the United Nations. Dad had told me about them. They go all over the world, he said, to stop people fighting. Perhaps they could come to us for a bit. Julie glared at me, then looked at David and then back to me.

"You won't tell? Either of you? You swear? On your life?"

She was such a pill. "Cross my heart and hope to die."

We both crossed our hearts. Mel didn't say anything. She'd probably lost the power of speech.

Julie smiled grudgingly at me. "Okay." I was going to get away with the fat cow thing. She must have been terrified. Nobody said anything for a bit.

Then David pointed to the pogo sticks. "You can't do this, can you?" I pointed to my two grazed knees. "What do you think?" He took one of the sticks from me. "Come on, I'll show you."

He was very good at it. He could pogo for miles and stop just like getting off a bus, no trouble. He pogoed all the way up to the clubhouse without falling off once. Then Julie kicked in. She showed us how to fall off without hurting ourselves. When she started to show Mel, I tugged at her sleeve and whispered, "Be nice to her because ..." and I knew everything was all right because she whispered back, "I know. She's sensitive." She made it sound like a disease, but she was back being Julie again and not some yelling banshee with stick out hair, showing her knickers.

We had a really good time in the end. We had a kind of relay race, David and me and Mel and Julie. And they won! Even though he was much better than anyone. I was a bit miffed at that, but David said we'd got to let them win because they'd both had such a fright. Then it started to get cold and Julie told us to go home for tea and she'd be back later. She also told us NOT TO TELL. We didn't. Not a word. But now, it wasn't our secret anymore. Mel knew. I told you, you couldn't keep anything from her. It wasn't worth trying. She would always find out in the end.

* * * * * *

At first I was a bit fed up that Mel had found out because the specialness of the secret - the sisterly sharing thing, just Julie and me, was gone. Somehow spread out between three people - well, four if you counted David and I suppose you had to - it sort of faded and disappeared. So that was sad, but it was also a relief because the awful responsibility of NEVER EVER SAYING THE WRONG THING was no longer just mine. And if we were together, and Mel and I were always together unless we were asleep, and quite often even then, we could cover for each other if the other one had a lapse. So although I felt miffed, it was actually a good thing.

Now we could talk about it together and we did. All the time. In fact, we hardly ever talked about anything else. We thought about them and wondered what they did and what it must feel like to be them. We wanted to know what it was like to have a man in your life who adored you. I began to envy Julie seriously because, although it must have been a drag getting dolled up every morning with all that stockings and suspenders and hair spray business, it was worth the effort because when he saw her walking down the street towards him his face went all funny and he smiled.

His normal, bit blank bit daft look vanished and he looked completely different. Not bored or sulky, but sort of glowing. I watched them together every morning from Julie's bedroom window and saw how they both seemed to become more when they were together.

I went into her room at first when she started going out so early because I was on the scrounge. I hoped she might have a lipstick that was nearly finished or an eyeshadow the wrong colour that she wouldn't miss. But then I saw them together and afterwards I went in to watch them. They seemed to be living at a different speed to everybody else. Like they were in a sports car when everyone else was on the bus. They laughed and talked and looked normal, but when they looked at each other they seemed to say more in the looks that lasted a minute than Mum and Dad did in weeks. It was very odd.

Mel and I watched them constantly. We wanted to know what it was like. I tried to include Mags. I asked her if she wanted a man in her life. But she just pushed a greasy strand of hair out of her eyes and ran her tongue along her braces so her mouth went all bulgy and said "No. I want to be a doctor first." And I thought that honestly if she was going to look like that for the rest of her life, and add a stiff white coat and one of those rubber things they wear round their necks, it was just as well because I couldn't imagine her ever getting one. Not like that. She'd have to do something first. Wash her hair or grow some bosoms or something.

Mel and I wanted one. We wanted a dreamboat - with jazzy clothes who could jump into a car without opening the door. Like Cookie in Sunset Strip. He was a real dish. Somehow we would have to get a car with no roof. That worried us because nobody we knew who wasn't on TV had one. Maggie said we'd have to take an umbrella if we wanted "to ride round in a convertible in this climate" or we'd drown. But we took no notice of her because she hadn't a clue. All she was interested in was diseases and people's insides. Hopeless, really.

We thought that if we were going to get a man we'd better keep a close eye on Julie and David to pick up a few tips. So we hid behind the practice wall in the early evenings to have a bit of a snoop. We went undercover, like "The Saint". We wanted to know what they talked about and what kissing was like. They never noticed us. Not once. Which was extraordinary because we made an awful racket. We whispered and giggled and I fell off the end of the wall once. I was too busy snooping and not watching what my feet were doing. And there was one time when he put his hand up her skirt and she sort of groaned and we had to stuff our hankerchieves in our mouths to stop us laughing out loud. That was terrible. I didn't know that your whole chest could HURT with not laughing. We had to run off quick to the far end of the gardens behind the club house before we actually dared laugh aloud. Because Julie would have killed us if she'd heard. Horribly. Then we lay down on the grass and howled. And just when I thought we were stopping, we only had to look at each other and groan a bit to make us start up all over again. It took us hours to get over it. No wonder Julie was on another planet. We were just watching her.

But even though it was sometimes very funny and deeply peculiar, we thought we should "wise up". That's what they said on TV. "Wise up, kid." On American TV shows anyway. We liked them best because they were funny and cool and the English ones were all about fat men in tights running about with

40

bows and arrows. Or Richard The Lionheart getting lost on his way home. I mean I ask you, what a twerp he was. I kept telling Mel history was about morons, but she wouldn't listen.

Anyway, now we had more important stuff to do. We had to practise our technique in case a man came along out of the blue. So we practised kissing Dr Kildare's photo - like they do on TV - lips pushed out, eyes closed - but that was no good because he got all wet and the photo was ruined. And they cost 3/6 in Woolworths those photos, so it was no joke.

After that we practised kissing with each other because we were free, but once Mel closed her eyes and said "darling" in a silly voice like she had a sore throat and I nearly wet myself I laughed so much. I only just made it to the loo. Then there was the other time I tried and she tasted of the fried egg she'd just had for breakfast. I was nearly sick, she tasted so awful.

Really, in the end it wasn't worth it. The whole thing was horrible. So we decided that the man would have to take charge of the kissing because otherwise I couldn't see it happening, to be honest.

* * * * * *

Every afternoon after school when it wasn't raining, we sat on the lookout seat on the rockery - Mel and me - and we waited. David appeared first because he got out of work earlier than Julie. He worked in an office. Julie told me he was an estate agent. I had to ask Mags what that was. She was the family encyclopaedia. This time she looked up from her book for more than a second. She chewed a strand of hair while she was looking. It was a bit off-putting because she looked at you very thoroughly, like you were some germ wriggling about under a microscope. She looked as if she could hear what you were thinking. She was seriously smart, Maggie, so you had to

41

be careful. One slip and she would know it all.

"Sally, what is it with all these questions? Are you trying out for Junior Criss Cross Quiz?"

She took the hair out of her mouth and it swung wet and heavy against her cheek. Horrible. I tried to look as if I hadn't a clue what she was on about.

"Course not. I just need to know, that's all. What IS an estate agent?"

She sighed so hard it was almost a moan. You could tell she thought I was the biggest drag in the universe.

"A man who takes your house and gets as much money as he can for it."

She went on writing her essay. I turned away so she couldn't see my face. I felt sick and sort of goose pimply. So that's what he was. A crook. I knew it all along. He didn't look daft, he looked shifty. There were people like him on TV every night.

They showed up out of the blue, always with those pointy shoes and thin ties, and then they took your house and turfed you out into the gutter. They took your money and your home. Just because he didn't wear a hat and live in Chicago didn't mean he couldn't be one. I went back to Mags for clarification.

"A sort of crook then?"

"That's one way of looking at it. It's not the most noble of callings. They just make money out of people, Sall."

She didn't even look up. She didn't have to. I got the picture. In America they were called the Mafia - here they put Inspector Lockheart from "No Hiding Place" on to it. He's an ace detective on TV and he drives round corners very fast in a car just like Dad's - until he catches you, and then wallop! The handcuffs go on and it's off to jail with you. For years on end. Forever - if you were bad enough. No wonder David was in such a paddy about his secret. Inspector Lockheart was probably onto him already.

Then it hit me. Julie had been sucked into it. A gangsters' moll - that's what they were called in the films - and all they ever got to do was scream and cry. Well, she could do that all right. Had years of practice at home. And they never told. That fitted too. She'd made us promise her just as she'd promised him. Oh Gawd luvaduck! She might even go to jail because of him.

That upset me, because although it would mean that I could have her room all the time, it would kill Mum and Dad. I mean, imagine their "firstborn" being taken away in irons by Inspector Lockheart. The shame would kill them. It might even stop Maggie being a doctor. I mean you couldn't exactly say, "Hello, I'm your doctor. My sister is a gangster's moll. You'll have seen her picture in the papers. Now, tell me where it hurts."

It was up to me now. The family had to be saved. I had to keep on their tail so that when Lockheart caught up with them, I could tell him. He looked a bit fierce with that prickly moustache and piggy eyes, but I'd just have to be very brave and tell him everything. I'd have to tell him that Julie was innocent. That she didn't know what David was up to because it was a secret. That she was really a good person and an ice skater who was nearly famous and brought us all lovely presents, even Mel, and she was the light of her parents' lives - being their firstborn. And she was far too pretty to rot away in jail chained to a wall.

She would have to cry then and so would I, but we'd have to do it nicely without stuff running out of our noses or he'd throw away the key. But if we got it right (and we'd jolly well have to), then his heart would melt and he'd let her go. But only after he'd told her how lucky she was to have a sister like me, who'd saved the entire family from ruin. So she really ought to give me her room in thanks. Forever.

I got a bit carried away here, but what was real was that Julie was in danger and it was up to me to stick together in times of trouble. That's what Mum said families were for.

So I did. I stuck to her like glue. I hardly ever let her out of my sight. Only to go to school. And by then she was safely in Heggartys and could hide behind the washing machines if Inspector Lockheart turned up before I could get there. I couldn't really see him marching into Heggartys to buy the latest record. He'd lie in wait for her outside. So on our way home from school, (the bus stop was just outside Heggartys), everyday we'd check to make sure he wasn't there and then go in to check on Julie. She was always very nice to us then. By four o'clock she was getting a bit bored. You could tell. She kept looking at the clock on the wall behind her. Counting the minutes until she could get out and see David.

We would sit on the stools for a bit and she'd put a record on for us and be so nice I felt bad about spying on her. But not for long because it was all for her own good. And it did liven things up a bit. Then we would go home for tea - usually to me, not Mels, because of Mum not working - and straight after tea we would be back out in the garden on the lookout waiting for David to go by on his way to meet Julie behind in the tennis club.

Now we knew, it was obvious he had something to hide. He kept looking around to make sure no-one was watching him, but we were. He always waved to us. The swine. And we always waved back because we didn't want him to twig that we were on to him. Then a few minutes later, Julie would come racing down the street. A bit late. She was always late.

Dad used to say that she'd be late for the last bloody judgment, but that was years ago when he had to take her to school. She drove him crazy then. That was before she became perfect. Mags and me went to the little school in those days. Just the mornings. Much better.

Now she zoomed by, you could tell it was her even without looking by the sharp click clack of her heels on the pavement. Hair all back-combed and sprayed, eyes and lips all made up, she did look nice. And always nicest of all for him.

She would smile at us and raise her finger to her lips to make sure we stayed silent. You could see she was worried. Terrified. One false move and she'd end up in a sack in a cellar. He must have done it hundreds of times before. There were probably bodies in cellars all over the place. But not this one. Not my sister. Mel and I were on the case and we'd hang on till the bitter end. Whatever happened.

We would watch her until she reached the end of the street and then we'd give each other the sign and, almost without talking, we'd follow her into the tennis club. We were going to protect her no matter what. We were sticking together, like Mum said, Just in case

CHAPTER 5

But there was one day we couldn't stick together. The day of the school fete. I was going with Mum and Dad in the afternoon. We were meeting Mel and her parents at the front gate. In the evening was the Juniors Dance. Maggie was going because she was in the Senior School. We were not going to the Junior's Dance because we were in the Junior School. Why they called it the Juniors' Dance I'll never know. They were all lunatics in that school. I did ask Miss Woodhouse if we could go, Mel and me, because we knew all about being grown-up because we had older sisters, but she turned me down flat. She said not to be silly, we were far too young, with that sort of snorty laugh that she usually saved for marking the spelling tests. She did that in front of the class, which was rather cruel, I thought. By the time she'd finished, mine was mostly red pen. But I wasn't the worst. Angela Humber was worse than me. Mel was rather good at it. She even came first sometimes. Sickening really.

Anyway, the Dance was no go for us. We were VERBOTEN. Mel and I had decided that Miss Woodhouse was an important Nazi left over from the War. She had the right temperament. She screamed and shouted and stamped about all the time. Honestly. All she was missing was the little moustache. She had the crazy glare and the need to hurt people. She had obviously sussed that Heathwood School For Girls was a good place to hide. With all the other lunatics.

It was sad about the Dance because they were going to have BOYS. Boys from Quainton Hall School had been invited and there were records (mostly supplied by Julie via Maggie) and dancing and fruit punch and sandwiches made in Domestic Science. And the pavilion was all done up with fairy lights outside and streamers inside. Like Christmas, only without the tree. It looked lovely.

We turned up for the fete early and had to wait for them to open the gates. Mel's mother had put her raincoat on which looked ominous. But Mel and I had made the effort with summer dresses and white sandals. We needn't have bothered. It was freezing and the fete was awful. It had rained the night before so the seats on all the rides were soaked and made you look as if you had wet your pants when you got off. Then it rained again heavily and the candy floss got so damp you couldn't eat it. Our shoes and socks got muddy and Mum and Mel's Mum gave up and went inside the pavilion. Dad tried to cheer us up by shooting one of those ducks that won't lie down even when they're shot and he won a prize. But it was only an old clock with gold paint on it that was peeling off already. You could see it was rubbish. He gave it to Mum, but she didn't look very pleased. What she did look was bored stiff but trying to put a good face on it.

We had saved up our pocket money for weeks for this. But all you could buy at the stalls were horrible book markers knitted by the Third Form and you could see where they had dropped the stitches. All the Victoria sponge had gone and the only other thing you could buy was rock cakes made by Miss Riley herself, which were made of rocks Dad reckoned. He stopped Mum eating one because he said he liked her best with teeth. They tasted horrible anyway. Probably poisoned.

In the end we left early. We wanted to see what was going on at home. Julie had been working on Maggie for weeks. Medicated creams, mud packs and eyebrow plucking (you could hear the screams even in the garden when she was doing that). The works. She had also been teaching her to dance in the living room after supper while Mum and Dad cleared up. Julie was a very good dancer and the lessons were tough. There was no messing about with Julie. She taught us to jive and even Quickstep in case Maggie needed it at the Dance. She said you never knew. It was good to be prepared. So Mags was prepared

48

all right, and funnily enough, she wasn't a bad dancer, even though she did it with a peculiar expression on her face. When she was concentrating, she went a bit boss eyed.

I tried to join in too, but they chucked me out after I jumped on the coffee table. Well, it was "Rock Around The Clock" so I thought things ought to get a bit lively. But I still had my shoes on. Julie was a Tartar, Mum trained, and she said she wasn't going to stand any messing about and she certainly wasn't going to be held responsible for any "damage" caused by me. So out I went, but I could still keep up with events because I used to peep through the keyhole. I could see Julie whizzing Maggie around the room. She could dance like grease lightning, Julie. I used to stay at the keyhole for hours, enjoying the music. I was getting rather good at this spying business. Perhaps I'd better be an international spy when I grow up.

I said as much at supper one night when Julie was going on forever about being a skater and Mags started up about how much she wanted to be a doctor. Dad made his usual speech (that we all knew by heart) about how all of us could do whatever we wanted as long as we worked at it because nothing worth having ever fell into your lap. Then he said he was sure Maggie could be a doctor if she worked hard enough, which was a bit daft because Maggie already worked harder than anyone else in the universe. I got up to get a glass of water, so I had my back to them.

"I think I'll be a spy when I grow up."

I couldn't see their faces, but I could hear spluttering.

"Good God, what will she think of next?" That was Dad in between chokes.

"I think I'd be rather good at it." I said, sitting down. Cool under fire, you see. Made for it.

Then Julie asked rather pointedly, "But can you keep a secret, Sally? Spies have to do that, no matter what."

"Even if they torture you," Maggie chipped in, " and in your case they probably will. I would." She was horrible these days.

49

"They'll have to catch me first." I told you I was good.

Dad winked at Mum and reached for the gravy. "Well, sweetie, I hope you decide against it. It's a very dangerous life."

"And not usually a long one. They'll shoot you at dawn, I expect."

I was beginning to hate Maggie. She wasn't my friend anymore. She was turning her sarcasm on me these days. She never did that before. But then I didn't talk to her like I used to on account of the secret. And I never waited for her at the bus stop anymore because of having to check on Julie. Perhaps she felt she was being left out, because she was. Poor old Mags. She always got spiky if you hurt her feelings. It was her defence, Mum said, because she hardly ever cried. But there was nothing I could do about it. I couldn't tell her because of being sworn to secrecy and I had to keep tailing Julie, to save her from ruin. Maybe one day Mags would understand. But she didn't now and it had spoiled things between us. We weren't allies anymore.

* * * * *

The day of the dance Julie took a half-day off work. Mr Heggarty must have hated it because it was a Saturday. But he wouldn't argue with Julie because she was "good for business". He told Mum that when she went in to complain about the spin dryer which had broken down again. It broke down all the time and Mum was always dragging dripping sheets and towels out onto the line and cursing Mr Heggarty.

Julie worked on Maggie all that afternoon. She had got to the hair by the time we got back from the fete. Shampooing and setting - we could hear the yells from the bathroom as we walked up the path. Julie had learned her hair washing skills from Mum. Heavy handed wasn't in it. Gestapo trained was more like it. Torture was going to be no obstacle to us. We'd

50

been brought up with it. Then the hair dryer droned away for hours. At first, we weren't allowed in. Then Julie relented and Mel and I were allowed in to watch.

Maggie sat on the stool in front of Julie's dressing table in her dressing gown staring at her reflection. She looked a real sight. Still red faced from the dryer, she had big rollers in her hair. They had metal spikes going through them so they looked a bit like Sputniks. "Earth to mother ship. Come in please. Alien monster on the loose." She looked horrible with her skinny old pipe cleaner legs stuffed into her Tony The Tiger slippers.

Anyway, then Julie began in earnest. You could tell she meant business. She brought her vanity case out from the walk in cupboard.

It was a lovely case, white leather lined with red silky stuff and a mirror in the lid. Mum and Dad had bought it for her last birthday before she went away. She had tons of make up in there. For ice skating, you see. First she put this pink stuff all over Maggie's face to hide the spots and then this thick beige stuff on top. You had to put that on with a sponge. It made Mags look really peculiar - her eyes and lips sort of vanished, but then so did the spots, so it worked. Then she did her eyes. Mum had gone on and on about that. Telling Julie not to make Maggie look "common". I'd have been a bit cross if I were Julie, but she wasn't. She just took no notice. She was good at that. Now she put a pale green shadow on Maggie's eyelids, and no eyeliner, just tons of mascara. Maggie looked pretty for the first time in her life. Mel and I couldn't believe it. Perhaps she did have nice eyes after all. Then Julie slicked a thin layer of pink lipstick across her lips and started to take the rollers out of her hair. It fell in fat curls around her face. She looked WONDERFUL. Mags stared in the mirror as if she couldn't believe it was her. I couldn't either. It didn't look like her a bit.

Then Julie gave her a little white lacy bra to wear and a sweet suspender belt to match. The stockings were thin and tan and she was going to wear Julie's shoes. Just for tonight. If they were too big, Julie said, she could stuff some tissues in the toes.

Oh, and while she was at it, she should stuff a few in her bra. Julie had it all sussed. Glamour was her middle name.

Then she went to the wardrobe. Julie had bought Maggie a dress for the dance, because it was her first she said, but she wouldn't show it to anyone. Not even Mum. Certainly not Mags. She took it out of it's cellophane bag and off the hanger. IT WAS FABULOUS. A beautiful, slinky dress with a little bolero to match that did up the back. In a sort of pale, ice blue that shimmered and shone and fell in soft folds that caught the light.

We went "Oh!" out loud, it was like magic, it was so wonderful. Julie said it was silk and looked for a minute as if she wished she'd bought it for herself. Then she saw Maggie. Maggie was just standing there in her stockings with her mouth open and her dressing gown undone. She looked at the dress and then she looked at Julie and her mouth opened and closed, but she said nothing. That was rare for Mags - talking was her thing. Usually she could do it. Julie looked at her and then at us.

"Maggie, what's the matter? Don't you like it?" She sounded a bit ragged because it must have cost her a fortune.

"Perhaps she's having a fit. You have to make her bite a spoon." Mel was only trying help. Julie looked as if she was going to tear her hair out.

Maggie tried to laugh but it was more of a sob. "Like it? … I ..." and two fat tears ran down her cheeks.

"Oh for God's sake, don't cry! You'll spoil everything, you stupid nit." Julie jabbed at Maggie's face with a tissue to stop the damage. Maggie hugged Julie as if she wanted to break every bone in her body. Drumming up business, I told Mel. It's what they do, doctors.

Julie put the dress on Maggie as if she were a doll and Maggie let her do it. She was speechless.

Julie zipped her up and said, "Now, remember, if you smile don't open your mouth or they'll see your braces." No Domestic Science sandwiches for her. She had to starve in the name of Glamour.

Then Julie did up the bolero and turned her round so she

could see herself in the mirror. It was staggering. The thing in the mirror wasn't my sister Maggie. This thing was BEAUTIFUL.

She didn't look boney and sort of gangly like a hung up puppet anymore. This dress made her look like she had a figure, which was very clever of it because she hadn't. Even her skinny old legs didn't look like they normally did, pipe cleaners in socks, but long and tanned and sort of elegant. The colour of the dress and the eye shadow made her eyes look green instead of muddy and she looked smart and grownup and sort of glossy. Like in a magazine.

Then she walked downstairs as if she was frightened she would break. Mel and I followed her down like a pair of bridesmaids. Julie came last carrying the Paris bag and her own charm bracelet which she said she would lend Maggie tonight "for luck". Didn't look to me like she was going to need any.

Mum and Dad were waiting in the living room. They were going to the dance too to help out with the food and drink. Mum had said she wasn't going to get "dressed up", but she'd put her best suit on. And her pearl earrings. When Maggie walked into the living room Mum gasped and Dad put the paper down and stood up. He was flabbergasted. All he could say was "wow" and grin like he'd gone daft. Mum beamed and nearly cried. (What was the matter with this family? She looked like a dream!) Then Mum raved about the dress.

"Julie - it's beautiful." She went up to touch it and stepped back as if it had burnt her."It's real silk!"

"Yeah" Julie was a bit embarrassed by all the fuss. "It's wild silk."

Then Mum turned on her. "How could you afford it?" Typical.

"I had some money saved up. And I missed her birthday and it's her first dance ..." Julie stammered.

She felt guilty for leaving her out of the secret. I could see that. But she didn't say that. So neither did I.

I kept staring at the dress. When Maggie moved, it sort

of swished softly. I loved it to die. I wanted one. Julie could leave me out of everything forever if it meant a frock like that. But no, all I got was her and her secret. Oh, and a rotten old Crunchie. It wasn't fair.

"You look beautiful, darling". Dad's voice was all soft and husky, the way men's go when they're trying to be gentle because they're terribly pleased with you. Dad was shocked rigid. You could tell. He'd never really thought of Maggie as a girl. I mean, she never liked dolls and she helped him fix the car and unscrew things and she knew about electricity and not getting wet. He'd thought of her as more of a boy. Well, she'd shown him now. She'd knocked his socks off. He kept looking at her as if he couldn't believe it. Well, none of us could really.

It was more than I could stand. "When is it going to be my turn?", I wailed.

"Never. If I can help it." Mum caught me in a bear hug. She was just like Mags. She could break bones.

Then Mum and Dad put Cinderella into the car as if she were made of glass and off they went to the dance. Julie went to get David. He was coming round in secret while they were out.

Mel and I were on strict orders NEVER TO TELL ON PAIN OF DEATH, but Julie promised to take him upstairs to play records in her room and leave the living room ALL to us for the whole time.

So Mel and I were left alone. We started to watch "The Sword of Freedom". It was still light outside. But we couldn't go out in the garden because of having to make the most of the living room. It was a bit dreary really. I wished I was going to a dance. I wished I was a painter or a sword fighter. I wished I was in Italy. I wished I was anything except on the sofa with Mel watching TV. Most of all, I wished I was Maggie.

* * * * * *

54

We fell asleep on the sofa with the TV on. I woke up and the Evening News was blaring away. My mouth was dry and my foot hurt from where Mel had slept on it. She was still asleep. Her mouth was open. She had dribbled a bit on the cushion. I went upstairs to go to the loo.

Not really awake, I climbed the stairs in the dark. No-one had turned the lights on. I was at the top of the stairs when I heard it. A rough, gasping sound. Really loud. It sounded like an animal in pain. Then it got louder and faster and more like crying.

I didn't go any further. I didn't want to. I knew Mum and Dad weren't home because they always kept the hall light on at night. For me - because I was scared of the dark. I still am.

The crying went on. I didn't know what to do. It was coming from Julie's room. I couldn't see anything because the door was closed. I could only hear. I didn't want to know what was going on in there because it sounded awful. Then there was a sort of a groan - and then silence.

I went back downstairs in the dark slowly. I would wait to go to the loo. I would wait until Mum and Dad got back. I wanted them back soon. I was very tired and I was fed up with everything being weird and a secret.

I wanted it to stop now. I wanted it to be like it was before. Cosy, always the same, a bit dull. Lovely.

I went back in to Mel and shut the door. She didn't wake up. Later, I think David went home because I heard the front door close. And later still, Mum and Dad and Maggie came back and the lights were turned on and they were chatting, but in whispers, and Maggie was all pleased and her eyes shone. She could tell me why in the morning. Mum and Dad were cross that we were still up. Mum made us go up to bed straight away and for once there was no fuss about brushing teeth. Just nighties on and into bed. I didn't see Julie. Perhaps she was asleep. I didn't go to sleep for ages. I couldn't settle. Sometime in the night I took my Teddy down from the shelf where I had put him because of me being too old for a teddy bear. I stroked his fur. It had worn away in places and he had only one eye and a wonky arm from where I'd been sick on him when I was little and Mum had washed him and his fur had fallen out. I put him in bed beside me. He felt soft and velvety except in the bald bits which I knew by heart. In the end, I fell asleep.

CHAPTER 6

The next morning everything went back to normal. Dad read the paper and grumbled about the government. Mum floated about for a while in her dressing gown and then started making noises about cooking lunch. Lunch was a bit elaborate in our house on Sundays. But Mags was very odd. She slept in late and when she did come down, she was all smiley and dead quiet. Not her usual spiky old self at all. She ate Cornflakes with Mel and me instead of Rice Crispies and didn't even seem to notice the difference. Maggie usually noticed everything. Her nickname in our family was "Hawkeye". Dad called her that when she was tiny because she didn't miss a trick. This morning she was missing everything. She didn't talk and she clearly wasn't listening when I spoke to her because I asked her for the strawberry jam and she passed me the Marmite instead, which she knows I hate. She just kept staring out of the window. It was dreadful. She didn't even read her silly old biology book. I kept asking her what was up, but she just shrugged her shoulders in a way that made me long to hit her and smiled her new idiots' smile and said calmly, "Nothing." I tell you the way this family's going, we'll all be in the loony bin by autumn.

When Mel went home, Mags told me all about the dance. It made me sick. Now even Maggie had a man. Everyone did except Mel and me. I wasn't sure how I felt about that now.

I mean, I wanted a man to jump in cars with and take me out and think I was beautiful. A man who would put down the paper and stand up when I came in the room with his mouth open, like Dad had with Maggie. Because I was so glamorous. I wanted the adoring really. But I wasn't that keen on the moaning bit - the lying on the grass with your skirt up, making a funny

57

noise business. I didn't like the sound of that. It sounded as if it hurt. Perhaps you could have a man without all that. Just for fun.

But now everyone in my family had one. Even though Mags' man had been temporary - for one night only - at least she'd had him. He gave her a rose from his buttonhole, a yellow one, and a cartoon drawing of Mickey Mouse that was rather good. He went to Quainton Hall School and his name was Richard Henderson. He wanted to go to art school and he had a racing bike. It was turquoise and silver and had special wheels. He told Maggie she was "lovely" and he asked her to have coffee with him in the Kardomah one day after school. She'd wanted to go, but she told him that she didn't think Mum and Dad would let her. Too honest, that girl. I'd have just gone and told Mum and Dad I was with Mel or something. Anything, but I'd have gone. But then I was like Julie. A born liar. After Mags told him it was no go at the Kardomah, he took her outside and they walked round the car park. He knew the names of all the cars. He was going to have a Ferrari one day, he said. Then he kissed her. He said perhaps they could get together later on when she was a doctor and he was at art school.

Then they went back inside and he drew Mickey for her on a paper napkin and wrote his phone number on the back. He said she could call him anytime if she wanted to talk. He said no one would object because there couldn't be any harm in that. And if she wanted to see him, she could always come to his schools' cricket matches because he was in the school team. The First Eleven. She said she might. So that was why she came home all smiley and pink. She showed me the rose and the drawing and then she put them away in her treasure drawer. He might be a famous artist one day, she said. It was enough to make you spit. Everyone had an admirer but me.

Julie didn't appear until lunchtime and even then she had black rings under her eyes. She told Mum she was "exhausted". And Mum fussed and clucked about her working too hard! That was rich. Mum told her to take it easy. She didn't know it, but it

58

was good advice. I looked at Julie carefully to see if there were any signs of him hurting her. She couldn't have been moaning and carrying on like that for nothing. But she seemed perfectly all right. No broken bones. A bit pale, but then she didn't have any make up on. She did wear a big jumper though, a "sloppy Joe". To hide the bruises, I expect. She ate an awful lot of lunch. Seconds of everything. Julie didn't usually have seconds, especially of pudding because she "watched" her figure. I'd have watched mine too, if I had one like hers. But today she ate and ate and then slept all afternoon on the sofa. Crazy. But at least he hadn't killed her. She was tough as old boots, that girl.

* * * * * *

After that Summer stopped playing "Will I? Won't I" and really began. It was May, the heat wave kicked in and suddenly everyone was out of doors. We went to the park as much as we could, but not as often as before because of watching Julie. There was a new dog in the park. He had dark red hair - the colour Mum calls auburn - and he was fabulous. Actually, he was called a Red Setter - I know because I looked him up in the "Observer Book of Dogs". This lovely dog let us stroke him and play catch the ball and his owner seemed a very nice man because he always let him off the lead and said Hello to us. They were both very friendly and not grumpy at all, so they were a big improvement on Mrs Braden and poor old Secundo.

Maggie started to sunbathe. She said the sun was good for her spots. Only she called it "therapeutic". You could tell she had begun an improvement campaign in case she saw Richard Henderson again. She took to sunbathing on the lawn after school. I hoped Richard Henderson wouldn't come by on his racing bike while Mags was at it because she looked really peculiar in her vest and knickers on the grass. You could see her ribs through her vest and she had no bosoms at all. Perhaps they were part of the plan. Perhaps she was hoping the sun would hatch them out like those baby birds in the incubator on "Zoo Time", while it was zapping the spots. A sort of two in one solution. Maggie always had a master plan of some sort or another on the go.

Anyway, she was a bit of a mixed blessing in the garden. She would lie very still and quiet with her eyes closed and she never wanted to talk or play. I did ask her, but she refused.

She was concentrating on her improvements I know, but I thought she was silly because playing would have helped to pass the time and I couldn't see how a really good game of Captain Cook could stop the sun's rays working. Actually, she was a nuisance because she cramped my style. She was hopeless at pretending. She laughed at me while I was discovering new worlds behind the greenhouse and putting down a mutiny in the rockery, and it put me off. So, now I only had the garden to myself very early in the morning and after supper when the sun wasn't hot enough for Mags. I made the most of it.

Dad was worse. He was in the garden less often, but he interfered a lot more. There were clumps of bright forget me nots all over the lawn, spilling over onto the paths and the flower beds. They were lovely. And then Killer Dad came along with his lawn mower and cut them all down. I protested. He said he couldn't just let the grass go on growing. I didn't see why not. It would be much nicer like that, all wild like in a jungle. And if it did get really long - like waist high - then no-one could see Maggie sun-bathing, which would be a boon, I thought. I appealed to Mum, but no one agreed with me. So all the lovely forget me nots and daisies and dandelions that made the lawn so pretty were mown down and replaced with those stupid stripes the mower made. Fortunately, they all grew back. Very quickly. Which served him right, I thought.

In the mornings the grass was still wet and the dew sparkled like diamonds on each tiny blade. Fat green buds reached out towards the sun like little hands. There were always

60

unexplored treasures. Beneath the trees, winged insects sheltered, balanced on the leaves, and in the evenings, when the shadows turned blue, the whole garden was full of danger. It was beautiful and new and it always took me by surprise. There were tiny flowers I hadn't seen before, and sudden flourishings of new leaves. I inspected my empire every day, in secret. Soon there would be ladybirds.

It got hot and then hotter. Dad brought the garden furniture out of the shed - the table and chairs and the long swing seat with the squashy cushions and fringed top. That was for them to have drinks outside and "enjoy the garden", but they hardly ever did. Even in this weather they stayed indoors. They only came out to do the gardening and then they went in again moaning about how their backs ached. They weren't interested really. Which suited me.

* * * * * *

One evening I was sitting in my crow's nest in the rockery, having a good think. It was a good hard think, but not a very cheerful one. School had gone badly that day. I had failed the arithmetic test for the third week in a row, Miss Riley had bawled at me in the playground for talking in line and, worst of all, in the rehearsals for the play (usually the best bit of school), I hit Elizabeth Earle. She crashed into me in the dance and she really hurt me. She was built like a gorilla, so when she crashed into you it was like running into a brick wall, so I hit her.

But Miss Roberts shouted at me and said if I couldn't behave, I'd be back on the cymbals. Which was where I had started at the beginning of term, until I began my charm offensive and told her how I loved acting and my sister was nearly an actress, being a skater, so it was in my blood, sort of. She took pity on me then and gave me the part of Third Gypsy, but she was really cross now and said she wished she hadn't. So I said sorry to Elizabeth, but I didn't mean it. Then Miss Roberts said she'd see me in her office in the morning after prayers, which didn't sound too good to me.

In my think I was wondering what I should be when I grew up. Acting was out if I couldn't stop hitting people. And if they were all going to be like Elizabeth Earle, I couldn't guarantee not to. I began thinking about everything. What I could be. Dad had told me to do that if I was in a jam. "Keep thinking, use your head, work out what you want and what you can do without." Even I knew you never got everything you wanted. Life was like Christmas, I decided, or those games at the fair where you work those funny metal claws and get a plastic duck instead of the diamond necklace you had your eye on. You had to grab what you could and wind up with some things you wanted and some you didn't. Then you had to learn to like what you'd got. It wasn't a very cheerful thought. I mean, instead of Richard Chamberlain or Efram Zimbalist Jnr and the mansion in Hollywood, you could end up with someone like David and being back on the cymbals. Life is very unfair.

The colour had all faded out of the sky and shadows were getting longer and the stone I was sitting on started to feel really cold. Mum put the lights on in the living room and I could see her and Dad through the window, sitting in their armchairs like two bookends, watching TV. Maggie was sprawled all across the sofa because I wasn't there to share it with her.

She was reading a book with her hands over her ears so as not to hear the television. She was very odd like that, she could have read in her own room, in peace and quiet, but she always said she liked it better downstairs because she liked " company", except she didn't have any because if you tried to talk to her she couldn't hear you and if you pulled her hands away, she kicked you. Well, she always kicked me. I don't suppose she would have kicked Mum and Dad, but then they didn't pull her hands away. They just left her alone. They didn't mind her being weird because she passed her exams. Always.

Julie was still out and her dinner was in the oven getting all dried up and crusty. I kicked one of the smaller stones, and then wished I hadn't because it started a sort of landslide and two more stones and some little plants went whizzing off down to the bottom. The insects under the rock were all running about in different directions, disturbed and upset. Some of them had been turned upside down and were just lying there, kicking their legs in fury. I knew how they felt. I felt the same myself.

"Bugger!" I like swearing. I get that from Dad. He swears sometimes, but only when Mum isn't around because she goes bananas.

"Bloody Bugger! Hells' bells!" I was working up to a "Sod it" when I was interrupted.

"What's up, Tink? Trouble in fairyland?" It was David on his way home.

A For your information -Yes. Everything's wrong. I can't do sums, I haven't got a man and I'm back on the cymbals because I thumped Elizabeth Earle."

"Flippin' heck." He climbed over the wall and then sat on it, facing me. Then he fished in his jacket pocket and got out a packet of Wrigleys' Spearmint gum. "You'd better have one of these." We each had one.

"Go on then. Spit it out." He can't have meant the gum because he'd only just given it to me.

"All right. I hate school. I'm not clever like Maggie or pretty like Julie. I'm just nothing."

"Er ...why should you be anything yet? You're still a kid."

"I can't be a kid all my life, can I ?"

"No. You can't." He thought for a moment. "Only one thing you can be."

"What?"

"Yourself. You're not like other kids."

Was I going to have to hit him too? He took one look at my face and hurried on. "I mean, you're quite a strong person, Sall. Nobody much pushes you round, do they?"

63

"Not if I can help it."

"That's what I mean. It's good to be like that. For later on. Nobody likes a stroppy kid, I grant you, but when a grown up won't be pushed around, that's a good thing, it's a sign of strength. You know, not letting people railroad you."

He was out of his depth here, but he kept going.

"I mean ... um... when you're grown up, you won't let other people make your decisions for you. It's not in your nature. That's good. Because if you do, it never works out - and you're the one who has to live with it. A He looked down the street and suddenly seemed as fed up as I was. "And getting out of it is..." He didn't even finish the sentence, but just sat there, looking miserable. We stared at each other bleakly for a moment. Then he shrugged.

"You'll be all right, Tink. It might be tough now, but it'll be better later on."

I wished he wouldn't call me Tink. It's short for Tinkerbell. From Peter Pan. Julie used to call me that when I was a baby because I didn't like people laughing at me. She said if people weren't nice to me, my light went out. Like Tinkerbell. She must have told him.

Suddenly he grinned. "Hang on a minute." And he was off over the wall, across the road and picking a tulip from Mrs Fisher's front garden! He had a terrific nerve, that boy. He came back and presented it to me with a sort of bow.

"Here you are, princess. From an admirer. Your first flower." He tried to ruffle my hair, but stopped short when he saw the expression on my face.

"You'll get a man, Sall. Just try not to frighten him to death. Okay?" And with that he was off. Heading for home.

* * * * * *

We were real friends after that. It had started with the Crunchie, but the flower showed he really did try to understand how I felt. I told Julie later that evening. I sat with her at the kitchen table while she ate her browned up meal. It looked horrible, but she didn't seem to care.

"That's him all over, Sall. He's so kind.... and dishy and funny and ..."

Slow down! Wait ! She'd left me behind.

She stared out of the window and then sighed and said, "I love him to die."

I knew she meant it. We only said that we loved something to die when we really meant it - the women in my family. You don't monkey around with that. Never know what might happen to you if you did.

"Don't look so worried. He adores you." She hugged me then and told me I was her best sister, even though I was only a kid. She told me we would always be close and that she would always do for me at least what she had done for Maggie. (She had seen my face when she brought out that dress!) Probably more because we were "Two of a kind" she said. Crooks and liars was more like it.

CHAPTER 7

The next day was rough. I went to see Miss Roberts. I told her what had happened - that every time we did the dance Elizabeth crashed into me because she couldn't tell left from right. Miss Roberts sighed and said she knew, but that it was no excuse for hitting people. She had no alternative, she said, but to put me back on the cymbals. Her decision was final. I begged and pleaded, but to no avail. I told her that it would make more sense to put Elizabeth on the cymbals because if she stayed dancing she would only crash into whoever else was next to her, so it didn't solve the problem. But Miss Roberts said very sharply that the problem was that I had lost my temper and hit someone, and for that there was "no excuse".

Then I cried a bit and asked her to give me a second chance because I loved being the Third Gypsy and I could actually do the dance. But she said No, no, no. So I had to give back the lovely black skirt with the coloured ribbons around the hem and my tambourine so someone else could have them. I went back to the classroom still crying and Miss Riley sent me out again to "pull myself together," so I sat in the loo and howled. Then dear old Mel came in and I told her everything, and she said she had always hated Miss Roberts because she wears laced up shoes like a mans'. Mel says you can tell a lot about a person from their shoes. And so did Sherlock Holmes, so she could be right.

Then she said that she had watched a lot of the play and she thought it was "really crummy", so just as well not be in it. She was only in the band herself, so at least we could be together. We stayed out for ages and then we ran the hot tap to steam up the mirror and played noughts and crosses on it. After a bit, Janet Elkins, the form monitor, came in and said we'd better get back to the classroom quick sharp because Miss Riley was getting cross and muttering that she doubted anyone who wasn't seriously ill needed to be the loo for that length of time. So it was back to the salt mines for us.

Apart from that, everything else was quite normal. Except Julie came home early. Too early. When Mum was getting supper and Mags and me were still doing our homework on the kitchen table. I liked that time. We were all very cosy together and I was making a big effort because I was going to show Miss Roberts how wrong she was. Mum liked us being "where she could keep an eye" on us and she liked us doing our homework too, so she was smiling. Peeling the potatoes for supper and humming a little song. Maggie was frowning because her homework was something called geometry which you do drawing with plastic things and metal spikes you stick a pencil in. Then you do the sums. It looked dreadful. I was tearing my hair out because although I liked the idea of astounding Miss Roberts, I couldn't actually do the sums. I hate numbers - they add up different every time. So when you try to check, you just get in a worse mess. Better race on through and never look back. Look what happened to poor old Lot's wife.

I had nearly finished when Julie came in. Her face was all blotchy and she looked as if she had been crying. She came in and glared at us as if we were all murderers.

I gave up on Simple Arithmetic. This looked a lot more promising. As usual, it was me that got the ball rolling.

"What's up?" She didn't answer. Mum turned round. "What's the matter, darling?" She never said that to me. "What's wrong now, Sally?" was more like it. Julie just stared at her. Mum tried again. "Had a bad day, love?" Julie burst into tears. Then she ran upstairs and we heard a door slam. Mum stopped smiling, dried her hands on the tea towel and went up after her. I was enthralled Even Mags was interested.

"I wonder what's up." I should have said nothing. I should have kept my trap shut. But no. If I were a fly, I'd march straight into that spiders web, no trouble.

Maggie put down her plastic circle and stabbed at the blotting paper with her metal spike. She called it a compass, but she must have got it wrong because it didn't tell you where you were. I haven't been playing Captain Cook all this time for nothing. She was thinking though, you could tell.

"I don't know..." then she looked up at me with her "I can turn you to stone" look. "I think... it's man trouble. Her boyfriend must have dumped her. You should know. You're always following her around."

God, what a brain! She could always have a think and take it further than anyone else. With nothing to go on, she'd already seen more than me! She was a genius. I tried to back pedal now because if she'd had a mind, she'd have got the lot out of me.

"Oh, I dunno. Maybe Mr Heggarty shouted at her. He shouts at everyone else."

"Yes, but never her. She wouldn't cry like that because of Mr Heggarty. She must be really hurt to cry like that. Specially in front of us."

She could be awesome, Maggie. Brain of Britain material. But luckily, she wasn't that interested. Feelings just didn't intrigue Maggie like they did me. She put her geometry back in her satchel and started a new subject. The nervous system of the frog. I told you she was a complete case.

I abandoned my homework all together. This was much more interesting. What had David said to her? Had he tried to kill her? Perhaps he had told her everything? About the Mafia. Perhaps she'd never see him again and die of a broken heart. It did happen. Mums' paperbacks were full of it. Or perhaps she'd have to go away and live in hiding, under an assumed name with a wig on, so that Inspector Lockheart would never find them. I could have her room then.

I hung around in the hall upstairs, but I couldn't hear

anything. Then Mum came out of Julie's room, looking a bit sad, and when she saw me she just shook her head and said. "It's no good, Sweetie. She won't tell me." Then she put her arm round my shoulders and we walked downstairs together. I was really worried now.

Julie didn't come down at all that night. When Mum went up to try and get her to come down for supper, she told her she had a headache, a migraine she called it. But you don't cry like that because of a headache. And she was crying. Hard. I heard her when I went up to bed. Sobs and gasps and a lot of sniffing. She could make a terrific racket, Julie.

Suffering in silence wasn't her style. She carried on like nothing on earth. I had to stuff my fingers in my ears and then go under the covers. Even then I could still hear her. So I went and knocked on her door. I said it was me and did she want a cuddle or a hot Ribena? But she didn't even open the door. She just sniffed extra hard and said "Go away, Sall." So I did.

The next morning she was out of the house before anyone was up. I heard the front door close when I was brushing my teeth. I spent all day wondering what was going on. Mel and I talked about it all though the breaks. I was so distracted that I shot a goal into the wrong goal post in netball. It was a jolly good goal, but I got boo'ed by my own side because I had scored it for the other team. I did say that I had family trouble, but they didn't care. They sent me to Coventry. Netball was everything to them. They knew nothing about men. They were such babies.

We raced out of school and onto the early bus to Heggartys. We feared the worst. She might not be there. She might have been taken off in an ambulance insane with grief. Or she might have started her new life - as Sylvia Richards or something - in a blonde wig. I hoped not. She'd look awful with those eyebrows. Julie's hair was really dark. Nearly black. Like Dads' was before he went grey. Could Lockheart have got her? We raced into the shop, past Mr H and his washing machines. He muttered something about not wanting "brats charging about in his shop" but I didn't care. Was she still there?

She was. Large as life and twice as normal. Cigarette on the go, sipping coffee from a mug. She even waved at me. I could have killed her.

"I've been worried sick about you all day long." I sounded just like Mum. That's what she could do to you. But she just smiled at me and put a record back in it's paper holder. "How sweet." Well, she wasn't going to smarm her way out of this one. Not with this sister.

"You tell me. Now. Go on. Spit it out." I liked that phrase. It sounded like I meant business. She looked a bit taken aback and then sighed. "Mix up, Sall. It's all okay now." She might have been okay, but I wasn't. "You made me score a goal in the wrong net."

"And it's the first goal she's ever scored." You could always count on Mel to stick the knife in. I decided I was going to murder her on the way home. Slowly.

Julie laughed. I was so angry I thought I was going to cry. She made me feel a complete fool. I dropped my blazer on the floor. Then she took pity on me. "I went to meet David and he didn't show up." She was whispering, so we had to kneel on the stools to hear her. "I thought it was all over." What did I tell you about Maggie? Then Julie smiled . "But it's all okay now. Just a mix up. Something came up and he had to go home."

Then she turned her attention to me. "Poor old Tink. Sorry about the goal. Here, have an ice cream on the way home." And she gave me the money for two cornets. She wasn't all bad.

When we were having our tea, the phone rang and Mum went to answer it. It must have been Aunty Ivy, because she was gone for hours. I kicked Maggie under the table.

"What now?" She didn't sound very pleased to be interrupted, but I had to get in quick before Mum came back. I thought if she had been worried like me, it was only fair to tell her something.

"You were right. I saw Julie on the way home. Boyfriend didn't show up. S'all right now. They've made up." I tried to

71

make it sound as if I didn't know anything much.

Maggie pulled a face. "Pity. Don't like the sound of him."

She didn't even know who he was. She was like Mycroft in Sherlock Holmes. Her thinking was a complete mystery. "Why? He ..." I had to think fast here and thinking faster than Mags was tricky. "...he...might be great. I dunno who he is, but he might really love her."

"Doesn't sound like it to me."

"Why?"

"Well," She sucked the end of her pencil, considering. Then she looked me straight in the eye. She had a terrible stare, Maggie, like those things that could turn you into stone. Lizard things. We were learning about them in Greek Legends. They were called Basilisks.

Then she pronounced sentence. "He was quite happy to let her think he'd dumped her. For a whole night. She was crying for most of it. I heard her. She was really cut up. He could have telephoned to put her out of her misery. Doesn't sound much like love to me."

With that she went back to her homework. Maggie always made everything sound so simple. Dad said she only saw things "in black or white." But the trouble was, she was mostly right.

* * * * *

My trouble was I didn't have Maggie's way with a problem. I struggled with it all for a few days and went round in circles. I tried to look it "from all angles" as Dad had told us to, but none of them seemed to make any sense. Was Maggie right?

She often was and yet she didn't know David, how nice he could be and how much he seemed to love Julie. And, most importantly, although she had been right about love upsetting

72

Julie when it went wrong, she had completely failed to notice how bright and shiningly happy he made her most of the time. And yet, he was a crook. I was convinced of it. His funny clothes, the way he insisted they should always be a secret, the way he suddenly looked sad for no reason. Because he knew he would probably spend most of his life in jail, I should think, and that he'd break Julie's heart by going there, in the end.

All these things were true. I had seen them all and yet together they didn't add up. It was very puzzling. Like having a very complicated jigsaw with bits that were missing or those awful bits of sky that fit in both ways, so you never get it right and see the whole picture. It makes your brain ache. I thought about it constantly and bullied Mel to keep thinking too, in case she got it first, but neither of us got anywhere.

After a few days, I decided that something had to be done, whether I understood or not, so the next morning I waited in the garden and waylaid David on his way to meet Julie.

"David!" He stopped in surprise. Usually, we just waved. I went up to the wall.

"I've been thinking."

"Steady on, Sall." I decided to rise above that.

"If you and Julie need me. And I think you do. To look out for you. Or take a message, like Mum does for Dad." He was looking even more daft than usual today, so he didn't twig.

"You know, to prevent a mix up. Like the other day. Well, I could do that. Because friends do that sort of thing, don't they?"

Finally the penny dropped, which was a good thing because I was beginning to feel a real lemon, standing there. Then he began to smile.

"Yeah. Yeah, they do. That would be smashing."

"What then? What should I do?" He didn't answer. He really wasn't the brightest pebble on the beach. Maggie would have been grinding her teeth by now.

"Well, you know my office is just round the corner from your school."

73

"I do now."

"Yeah, Harris, Lambert & Iverson, the estate agents. If you could pop in on your way home - just for a second, I could tell you if it's okay or not. Then Julie would never have to... well, get all upset like the other day, because you could tell her if it's on or not when you see her at Heggartys. You do that every day, don't you, Sall?"

I do now, Mister, because I'm trying to keep her out of jail, thanks to you. But I didn't say that because of Mrs Fisher's tulip. I only thought it.

"Would you do that for us?"

"Nothing simpler, my dear Watson."

I was reading Sherlock Holmes with Dad, because he loved it and said it would "ginger up" my brain. If only he knew. My brain didn't need gingering up. It was in overdrive already. But I thought it was a good quote for a secret messenger who was also a spy. I put out my hand to shake.

"You can rely on me."

"Sally, you are a cracker." And he kissed my cheek! Very lightly and a bit like Dad, but still a kiss from a boy! I was coming along now. No-one of my age I knew had been kissed by a boy.

All right, it wasn't a proper kiss with lips and closed eyes and everything, but you had to start somewhere. I went into school that day feeling like a million dollars. So what if I was back on the cymbals and scored goals in the wrong net? That was only for babies, anyway. My real life had begun. I was going to be a beautiful film star, in Hollywood, with high heels and men kissing me all the time. I knew it. I was already a spy and a secret agent and I wasn't even in Senior School! I was going to be terribly important And it had all started today.

* * * * * *

It was just as well the new life had begun because the old one was becoming a bit of a challenge - what with being back on the cymbals and still being in Coventry except for Mel. So I concentrated on the secret agent business because, frankly, it was going better.

The next day, we put into practice my secret messenger plan and called in on David on the way home. I included Mel in the plan. Well, I had to. She was always with me.

I could hardly say - "Hang on, Mel. Just in popping in to buy a house." Could I? I couldn't have left her out of it if I'd tried. So I didn't.

Anyway, disaster struck. Again.

We called into Harris, Lambert & Iverson on our way home as requested and waited in the reception area until David came. It was very snazzy in there. Fancy glass tables with magazines on and two purple furry sofas and a spiky looking plant in a bin. It was taller than me. We asked the girl in reception for David. She looked at us as if we were something Secundo might do in the garden. She was horrible. She had chipped nail polish and crusted up make up over her spots to hide them, only it didn't - the make up had all run into the scabs so she looked like the Creature from the Black Lagoon. She didn't think much of us either. I said David was expecting us and she said "Crikey" and her painted on eyebrows disappeared into her beehive and then she sort of laughed.

She rang through to tell him we were there. She didn't ask us to sit down or say he wouldn't be long or anything secretaries are supposed to say. I didn't expect her to understand our mission, but I did expect manners. What Mum called Common Courtesy. Well, she hadn't got any. Then she scratched her head with her pencil, so what she probably had was fleas.

David came down, all smiley and a bit red-faced and said "Nice, isn't it?" meaning his office. And it was, except for the Creature Time Forgot in reception. She said nastily "Bit young, aren't they - even for you, Dave? 'Bye 'bye, kiddies. Have fun."

And she turned back to her typewriter. She had dandruff all over her collar. Honestly, she was like one of Captain Cook's crew after they'd run out of the lemons.

I closed my eyes and had a quick imagine of making her walk the plank, but not for long because I was on a mission. Then David said it was okay for today, so we left the office. On the bus on the way home, I took off my blazer and wore it over my shoulders with no arms in because I was practising for Hollywood and the fur cape. All film stars had those. Mine was going to be white. Ermine probably. Like the Queen.

When we walked into Heggartys, Mr Heggarty was busy with customers so he couldn't moan about us. He was showing a fat looking girl and an older woman his range of twin tub washing machines. The older woman looked like a real Battleaxe. She had dyed blonde hair with black roots and terribly thin lips.

Anyway, she was giving old Heggarty a run for his money, so she can't have been all bad. She made him open up every single washing machine so she could see inside and then she sat down on the chair by the counter and read through the brochures. All of them. The younger one looked a bit embarrassed. The Battleaxe was probably her mother. We went up to Julie and I told her all about David and the offices, but she wasn't listening. She was staring at the two women. Mostly at the girl. I couldn't see why. She looked perfectly ordinary to me. Straight brown hair, baggy sort of dress. A bit fat. Nothing to gawp at.

"Stop staring. It's rude."

"I'm not." She went scarlet and put a LP record back in the wrong cover. Then she started staring again.

Mel and I went up to read the weeks' Top Twenty Chart which pinned up on the wall. My only chance to get out of Coventry was to be in the know. If I could tell them what was in the Top Ten I might recover my standing. Especially if I wrote it out so I could hand it round the class. Perhaps Julie would let me do it now, so there would be no mistakes. I went to ask her.

She was still staring.

"You're very rude. There's nothing to stare at."

She didn't move her eyes away for even one second. She looked stupid, like someone was brainwashing her.

"Oh yes there is." Her voice sounded shaky. At that moment the girl, who was probably dying to get away from her mother, saw Julie and her face split open in a smile. For a moment, she almost looked pretty.

"Jules! You're back!" She made her way across to us, squeezing past the machinery. The shop was like an obstacle course for her. She really shouldn't be that size at her age. Julie didn't say anything. She looked like a rabbit caught in a car's headlights.

"Who is she?" I hissed at her. She had reached us now.

"Jeannie - how are you?" It didn't sound like Julie's voice at all. Julie's voice was different to other peoples, it was plummy and low and a bit show bizzy. This voice sounded as if she had bits of glass in her throat. Jeannie didn't seem to notice anything wrong.

"Oh, I'm fine. On top of the world. Look at me - I'm the size of a house", she clambered awkwardly onto one of the stools. "Won't be long now. I'm sure it's a boy. He kicks all the time. David says I must have Danny Blanchflower in there." Then she laughed as if she was really happy.

Still Julie said nothing. It didn't matter. Jeannie was rattling on for both of them.

"So, Jules," She hated being called that. A We both got what we wanted. Remember at school - that break we were kept in because of the rain - and we all sat around and said what we wanted to do with our lives? And you said you wanted to be a skater - and you are. We're so proud of you. David kept the local paper when you were on at Wembley. It was a lovely picture they had of you. And I said I wanted a baby! Didn't think I'd get one quite so quick - but you know David. Never one to hang around. Mr Speedy Gonzales himself. This little one was on the way, so we got married quick and moved in with Mum."

77

She must have been uncomfortable because she kept shifting around. The stools weren't meant for someone that size.

"I never thought I'd end up with him. To tell you the truth, I always thought you and he were an item. Funny how life works out, isn't it? I expect... oh!"

Jeannie stopped talking, her face changed and then she smiled a kind of distant smile as if she was listening to a music no one else could hear. "OH! There he is! Feel!" And she grabbed Julie's hand across the counter and put it on her stomach. I watched Julie's face turn red, then white, then a sort of grey, like putty.

"See what I mean?" Julie nodded.

Jeannie heaved herself off the stool. "Must rush. Got to get this washing machine sorted out. Don't want to do without one now! See you soon. Come round and see us." And Julie smiled as if her face might crack and Jeannie lumbered off back to her mother and Mr Heggarty.

As soon as she disappeared behind the fridges, Julie ran into the stock room and out the back. I went round the counter and followed her, telling Mel to hold the fort.

I found her sitting on a dustbin out the back where Mr Heggarty put all the old cardboard boxes and bags of rubbish. She was crying her eyes out. Again. I handed her my school serviette. It was only a bit dirty. I was bringing it home for Mum to wash. It was no good giving her a hankie. It would never be up to the task. Even if I could find it.

She took the serviette and blew her nose. Then she looked at me. She looked awful - all snotty and red eyed, and her mascara
had run in smudgy black lines down her face. Then it was her turn to talk.

"I knew he'd married Jeannie - I heard it on the grapevine. But nobody told me it was a shot gun wedding." She sniffed then and sounded angry.

I didn't know what she was talking about. Shot gun wedding - did he shoot someone? Or did his friends just bring

78

their guns? They do that sort of thing in the Mafia. Must have been a bit of a shock for the Vicar.

Julie went on, her lips wobbly. "He never told me she was having a baby. He told me it was all a mistake. That he'd married her on the rebound because I'd gone away. He did ask me not to go, you see, Sall, but I was so crazy to be a skater ... I thought he'd wait for me."

She started to cry properly now. "When we met up again, he said he'd always loved me. He said he'd leave her - sort everything out. But he never told me ... Oh God, Sally, I felt it move!" She was really bawling now. I hoped noBone could see us. I looked around to make sure no-one was watching. But she just went on and on. As if she knew no-one could sort this out I just let her cry. I didn't know what else to do. I just stood beside her and held her hand.

When she'd finished, she blew her nose hard on the serviette and looked at me. "It's such a mess, Sall. It'll never be right now."

I could see what she meant. Leaving Jeannie was one thing, walking out on a baby was another. He couldn't just up and do that. But if he didn't then sooner or later, he'd have to up and leave Julie. He couldn't have both. It was either/or. Whichever way he went, he was going to hurt someone. Badly.

She was right. It was an awful mess.

I was out of my depth here. I longed to tell Mum. But I knew I never could. Because this was serious now. I could only tell Mel and I made her swear on the way home NEVER EVER to divulge on PAIN OF DEATH. I was beginning to sound like Julie now. If that was what love can do to you, I think I'll do without it.

I needn't have worried about Mel. She was so shocked she was struck dumb. She didn't say anything. Not even to me.

We decided not to go straight home, so we went for a walk in the park to see if it would help us sort things out. It didn't. We walked through the woody bit and past the bowling green and down to the stream but it didn't seem to help. Then the Red Setter came running up to us across the grass and his owner waved. We waved back and then sat down on a bench. The Red Setter wanted to play, he kept bounding off and then waiting for us to run after him but we couldn't. We were too upset. So he came back and sat beside us.

"What's up with you two? You look as if you've lost sixpence and found a penny!" The owner sat down beside us. It was a bit squashed up so we moved up to make room for him. Then the Red Setter put his head on my knee. He really was a lovely dog.

"He seems to have taken quite a shine to you. By the way, my name's Tim and he's called Rusty." He smiled at me and I tried to smile back. I couldn't really manage a conversation but I told Tim our names. It would have been rude not to. Nobody spoke for a bit.

"You two really are in the dumps." There was no arguing with that.

" You know if you're in some kind of trouble, you can always tell me. That's what friends are for." But I couldn't tell him because he wasn't a friend. We hardly knew him.

I didn't know what to say so I stroked Rusty's head and his long silky ears. He looked up at me as if he understood everything. Then Tim put his arm round my shoulders and sort of squeezed me. I didn't like that, so I moved away a bit. I didn't say anything. Then Tim stood up and winked at me, "Cheer up, Popsy. May never happen." Little did he know. It already had. "See you again soon." He walked away and I felt awful. He had only been trying to be nice and perhaps he was lonely. Rusty stayed with us.

Tim turned around " You've got the magic touch, Sally. He wants to stay with you." And I wished he could. But I smiled at Tim extra nicely and I said I hoped we would see them both again very soon. Because he had tried to be a friend. He waved and walked away and this time Rusty followed him.

We walked back very slowly and then we sat on the garden wall for ages. I didn't want to go in. Because if I did I'd want to tell. Mum or even Mags. But even Mags couldn't work her way out of this one. It was up to me to shut up and stick to Julie. Whatever occurred. But it didn't look hopeful. Whichever way you looked at it, it was a complete mess.

* * * * * *

When I did go in, I cracked immediately. I went to see Mags. She was in the garden, improving herself. I left Mel with Mum to make the banana sandwiches. She wouldn't notice if Mel was a bit quiet because she always was. But I needed to see Mags to get something straight in my mind because it was buzzing round in my brain like an angry bee.

I went to Mags for information. Also for comfort, because with everything so muddled up and awful, she could be very reassuring. She never got rattled. In a world where everything was turned upside down and no-one stayed in the same place - she did.

She was sunbathing, so she wasn't very talkative, but I didn't let that bother me. I wanted facts, not chat. And facts she would always give me because Maggie only dealt in facts.

" Mags?"

" Urgh...what?" She opened one eye because the sun was in her face. It was all screwed up. She was beginning to go red. She didn't look very inviting.

" What's a shot gun wedding?"

" One you don't ever want to have."

She closed her eye and went on improving. Not very helpful. But I was on a mission so I had to persist.

" Why? What is it?" I stood between her and the sun so that she was in my shadow. I felt very frazzled. She opened both eyes this time.

" It's when a man is forced to marry a woman because she's pregnant." She was cross with me. " You do ask the weirdest questions, Sally."

I should have guessed. I sat down on her towel with a thump. She tried to kick me off.

" What's it to you? Not pregnant, are you? You haven't even got a boyfriend." She laughed at me. That made me really cross. I was upset because of Julie anyway, and having to keep the secret, but suddenly I felt really cheesed off with Maggie. With her having a man and passing her exams and always being right. I don't much like people who kick me, either. And the teachers at school were always saying, " Why can't you be more like your sister, Sally?" Well, I was going to be like my sister. The other one. The gangster's moll. I decided to start my life of crime right now.

So I got hold of the end of the towel and stood up. Then I yanked it really hard and Maggie went rolling off into the rose bed. " OW!" She wasn't laughing now. Then I ran for it. " I'll get you for this!" She would too. But as I turned round and watched her pick bits of rosebush out of her knickers, I thought it was worth it.

So much for comfort from Maggie. Families were a dead loss these days. I wondered what it would be like to be an orphan. I guessed lonely, but free from aggravation.

I went in for my banana sandwich. Mum had gone upstairs, so Mel and I had a conference. She still looked a bit alarmed. I knew how she felt.

We decided to keep on trailing Julie and David in case she killed him. Then we could get her away into hiding before Lockheart pounced. Where I didn't know. Mel offered her garden shed, which was sweet of her, but I didn't think we could rely on Julie to keep quiet and out of sight. Her feelings seemed to require a lot of noise, and if she ever had cause for making a racket, it was now.

So we went off to the tennis club, but we were a bit late. They were already there before us. Sitting on the grassy slope by the practice wall. Julie was very upset, I could see. She was waving her hands about. David just sat there, all huddled up, pulling out tufts of grass. We crept up to the other side of the wall and listened.

" How could you not tell me? You're having a baby for God's sake! " she wailed. Then she breathed in with a sort of sob. " I don't know how you could do this - to Jeannie or to me. I don't think you love anybody. I don't think you can. I hate you." She scrambled awkwardly to her feet and for a minute, it looked as if she would fall. Her thin, spiky heels were all wrong for a grassy slope.

" I don't ever want to see you again." Then she walked away, all wobbly, with as much dignity as she could muster. It wasn't much. He didn't say anything. He just looked after her as she walked away and then put his head on his hands, resting them on his knees. His legs looked very thin in his drainpipe trousers. For a moment, I thought he'd gone to sleep.

Then he cried. Awful, gulping sobs that sounded as if he couldn't breathe. I had never heard a man cry before. Dad never did, but then he had no reason to. David cried out loud. I had never seen anyone look so unhappy in my whole life.

I turned to Mel. Her bottom lip was all trembly, and I suspected mine was too because my throat was tight and my eyes were beginning to sting.

She said, " We should go now." She was right. I held her hand and let her lead me away. She was very good with other people's feelings, Mel. It was because she had too many of her own.

* * * * *

We walked round to Mel's house. The blossom had fallen off the trees. It lay in drifts on the pavement, like confetti. I didn't want to go home. Be subject to scrutiny. I wasn't up to it.

83

So we went to Mel's where her Mum would be busy working and leave us alone. Mel's sister Maddy was there. She was painting a picture. The breakfast room table was covered with newspaper and her painting things. She was painting some flowers in a vase. It was very good. The leaves looked thin and veiny and the petals had tiny specks of pollen on them. It was much better than Richard Henderson's Mickey Mouse. Perhaps she was going to be a great artist too. She'd made a jolly good start. Anyway, she was too busy to bother with us. Except she did help us get the biscuit tin down because they kept it on a high shelf in the pantry. To keep the Mel out I suspect, rather than the mice. She was very fond of biscuits.

Maddy did say, " You all right, Sally?" and when I asked her why, she just said " You seem a bit quiet, that's all." So she did notice things, but she didn't push it like they would have done at home. They were all sensitive in that family.

CHAPTER 8

Then Mel's Mum came in and told Maddy to clear up now because she was going to make tea. They had tea later than us so sometimes, if we timed it right, we had two. We helped Maddy put the paints away and she showed us how to clean the brushes with turpentine. It smelled awful. Even worse than Aunty Peggy's scent.

Maddy painted in oils. No one else I knew did that. We all splashed about with water colours, but she had lovely little tubes of oil paint and she squidged them out in blobs onto a funny looking wooden tray called a palette. No khaki trees for her, no runny colours, no dirty water jar - just blobs of clear, bright paint. It was wonderful.

Anyway, then Mel's Mum put the tablecloth on and said did Mum know where I was. No, she didn't, because I hadn't told her. I had forgotten to tell her. We had just gone. Mel's Mum said I had better phone her at once. I did. Maggie answered.

" Ooooh, Sally. Are you in trouble!" She was really rubbing it in. She was still cross about the rosebush.

Then Mum came on the phone.

" Sally! Where are you?" She sounded more frightened than cross. I told her. Then came the cross bit.

" I've been worried sick about you. Walking out like that! Where have you been?"

" Mel's."

Then the axe fell.

" Why didn't you tell me where you were going?"

" I forgot."

" Oh, did you? I'm really cross with you, Sally. I'm going to have to tell your father." I didn't see why. But she always wheeled him in when she was in a lather. He was her biggest weapon. Her own personal A bomb.

" I want you to come home right away. No, you may not stay to tea. You've already had tea. You come straight home NOW." Then came the threat. " And if you're not here in ten minutes, my girl, I'm coming to get you."

Oh Gawd luvaduck! She was in a real snit now. Mum didn't get angry often, but when she did, she stayed angry. It took her days to calm down. Very long days.

So I told Mel's Mum I couldn't stay. Mel walked me back halfway round the circle. There was no sign of David. I hoped he hadn't killed himself. Or anyone else. You never know with criminals. They can go on the rampage when things go wrong.

* * * * *

When I got home the atmosphere was awful. Mum spoke in that horrible, crisp voice she reserves for punishment purposes only. Maggie was smirking. I hated her. I was glad about the rosebush. I asked if I could have a drink and Mum said, " Do what you want, Sally," in her best " I wash my hands of you, but just you wait 'til your father gets home" tone of voice. Then she wouldn't speak to me.

It was beginning to get me down. Coventry at school, now Coventry at home. I was starting to feel like the Count of Monte Cristo Soon I'd be tapping on the walls for company. I poured myself a glass of milk and I was so upset I spilled some. Then Mum shouted at me, " You stupid child! Now look what you've done!" It ran in a sort of pool across the table towards

Maggie's homework. I knew if I ruined that it would be me for dissection and not the frog. So I grabbed the tea towel to mop it up quick before it made her isoceles triangle run.

Maggie lifted up her papers and the milk ran past her onto the floor. Then I bent down and mopped it up, but Mum screamed at me again, " Not with the tea cloth! Not on the floor! Oh, for God's sake, Sally, just go to your room and stay there!"

I went to my room and shut the door. Then I got Ted down from the shelf and burst into tears. What was the matter with everybody? The whole world was going mad. Shot gun weddings and crooks and girls with babies. And people marrying people they didn't love and having to ditch those they did. I didn't understand any of it. And the crying - everyone was always in tears now - even me. And Mum had gone beserk and Maggie hated me and Julie had a broken heart.

I hadn't been able to save her at all. It had all been a terrible failure. Nothing was right. The mission had foundered and it was all my fault. It must be. If only I could have thought of a way to make things better.

The door opened a crack. Maggie peered round it. I wiped my eyes and nose with my hand. She pulled a face and came in. Then she handed me her handkerchief. She always had a clean handkerchief. She was that sort of girl.

" I'm still cross about the rosebush."

" I know." It was one of the reasons for my misery. One sister hated me and the other was on the verge of ruin. Mum wouldn't speak to me. My plan to stick the family together had worked a treat, hadn't it? I cried even harder now.

Maggie came and sat on the bed. " What's the matter with you these days? You've gone bonkers."

I couldn't tell her why.

" I don't understand."

" What don't you understand?"

I had a good sniff. " Anything."

" You are such a goose, Sally Palmer." Then she wiped my eyes with her handkerchief. " Stop it. Here. Blow your nose.

Nothing's that bad. So you went to Mel's without telling Mum? Bit daft, but so what? Doesn't exactly make you Adolf Hitler does it?" She was making me feel better already.

" What shall I do?"

" Tough it out. You know the score. She'll be cross. He'll huff and puff because she's told him to. Then it'll blow over. Like always. And," she stood up now, " although you are a ROYAL PAIN IN THE NECK, you are not quite the devil himself. So stop wailing." She gave me a quick hug and I clutched at her as if I were sinking in the swimming pool. She prised me off. Maggie didn't like what she called " people mauling her." Not even Mum. She walked to the doorway, then she looked back.

" But don't think you've got away with the rosebush. That's unfinished business."

And with that she went. She was weird, Maggie, but terribly comforting because although you couldn't get away with anything ever, at the same time, when she became what she called " an ally," she was one for keeps. She didn't waver the way Julie or I would have done. Dad said she was a " cool customer" because if she was punished for something she said she hadn't done, she would never say sorry for the sake of a quiet life. She'd rather die first. You could do anything to her. Smack her, keep her in her room for days, stop her pocket money, anything. She didn't care. She was bully-proof. She would get me for that rosebush, but she'd never kick me when I was down. She'd wait until I was back on my feet. She had a kind of honour, really. Like the Knights of the Round Table.

When Dad got back, I was sent in to see him. He was in his study. That was a bad sign. We hardly ever went in there. It had a desk and all his papers and books no-one ever read. It was just him and me. That was also bad. Only serious punishment took place in private. Usually misdemeanours were dealt with in public.

" I hear you've disgraced yourself, Madam." He sounded very stern. I didn't say anything. It was best not to.

" Your mother was frantic. I'm surprised at you, Sally." Funny how he was always surprised when we were bad. You'd have thought he'd have got used to it by now.

" You know better than to run off like that without telling anyone." Then he looked down and his eyes wrinkled up a bit.

" However, I have received an intervention on your behalf." Hoorah! That was Maggie spiking the guns.

" Who tells me that, although you are ...and I think the precise phrase was " a pesty kid", you have, apparently, been having a hard time of it lately. I don't remember all the details, but gypsics and cymbals came into it somewhere." He was definitely trying not to smile now.

" Oh yes, and goals in the wrong net." He sighed. He took a dim view of that. Then he looked up at the mantelpiece where all his silver cups were. He'd won them at school. For sport. We never won anything. Not one of us. He was probably wishing he'd had a son. He was probably wishing he'd had a gerbil. Anything except a daughter like me.

Then he looked at me and shook his head. " For God's sake Sally, be a good girl and don't upset your mother. She gets a bit rattled if she thinks you've vanished off the face of the earth." You could see where Maggie got the sarcasm from.

I sniffed a bit and said " Yes, Dad. Sorry."

" No good saying sorry to me. Go and tell your mother. Go on - give her a hug, grovel a bit and tell her it's no pocket money for two weeks. That should keep her happy. "

" But not me", I muttered.

He heard. " What did you say?"

" Nothing." I knew better than to argue with him.

" Good. Because at the moment, Madam, your happiness is not my paramount concern."

It was hopeless. Life was impossible and it was not going to get any better. Not in the short term, anyway. I walked towards the door, dragging my feet.

Then he relented. " However, if you behave, and if your

mother tells me you have been a paragon, an absolute paragon, mind you, we can review the situation. In a week."

And I knew then there was room for negotiation.

Julie did not come home that night. But she was not in disgrace like me because she rang and said she was spending the night with Pauline, one of her skater friends. She lived in Swiss Cottage, in her own flat in town. But I didn't know how Julie was and I worried about her. I worried about David too.

CHAPTER 9

The next morning I got to school early on account of there being no David or Julie to watch. It was a lovely morning. Bright and sunny with a deep blue sky and little white fluffy clouds racing along as if they were too busy to stop.

The first lesson was French which was terribly boring. I kept looking out of the window at the lilac tree in the playground. It was covered in deep purple blooms and smelled heavenly. Even in the classroom with it's stink of chalk dust and old socks, you could smell it if you sniffed hard. I must have been doing a lot of that because Mrs Barnes, our French teacher, spoke to me.

" Stop sniffing, Sally. Blow your nose. Have you got a cold?"

" No, Mrs Barnes. It's hay fever." That would fox her. I rummaged for my handkerchief. As usual, I couldn't find it. Why did hankies get themselves lost all the time? Mel was glaring at me because she really did have hay fever. In the summer she was always sneezing and her eyes went all red and puffy. So she was a bit possessive about it. But anyway, Mrs Barnes can't have believed me because she said,

" Really? Perhaps you'd like to tell me what that is in French?"

Fat chance! I barely knew what it was in English. I must have looked a bit panic stricken because she moved on.

" I thought so. Just pay attention, will you, Sally? Your command of the French language is not so accomplished that you can afford not to listen."

She always spoke like that. Long words in even longer sentences that you had to struggle to understand. It was like untangling knots, a conversation with Mrs Barnes. Best avoided. I put my listening face on.

She droned on and on. Trying to whip up some enthusiasm in the class for this drip called Sandrine, who was coming to our school on a kind of exchange. Apparently, all she wanted to do in her " sejour a Londres" was ride on a double decker bus and watch the Changing of the Guard. You could tell what she was going to be like.

Anyway, Mrs Barnes was trying to din a few simple phrases into us so that when she arrived we could say, " How are you? It is raining today. Do you know the way to the station? Do you like hard boiled eggs?" Honestly. What a conversation that was going to be.

It was pitiful, really, and even more so because, although we had to pretend we were all agog to meet Sandrine (or Mrs B would have flayed us alive), none of us actually wanted to say the words out loud in case we sounded even more daft than we already were. Which took some doing. Caroline Harris was a case in point. She was built like a rugby player, but she had no brain. Truly. None at all. Mel's cat, Sooty, was brighter than Caro, and she got lost if you let her out into the garden. You had to go and fetch her because she couldn't find her way back. But she was like Brain of Britain compared to Caro.

Mrs Barnes was getting cross. She kept tapping the board cleaner and little clouds of chalk dust rose up into the air each time she did. It was settling all over her navy blue jacket.

You could tell it was going to be a very long morning. I wondered where Julie was. If she'd turned up for work at Heggartys or not. And David? What kind of a state was he in? He was only down the road. Perhaps I could try and sneak out at lunchtime to see him. I had never done that before, and I think the school stood you in front of a firing squad if you were caught, but I'd just have to be careful. I was a secret agent, after all.

At last the bell rang and we were rescued. At last! Normally, I loved break. It was a good chance to run about, munch a few sweets and catch up on the gossip. But, at the moment, it was a bit grim. No-one would let me skip with them and gossip was off because of Coventry. Mel had offered to share my Coventry with me, which was good of her, so we sort of trailed round on our own.

I noticed that Deborah kept looking at me. That made me nervous. Deborah Rees Jones was our doctor's daughter. She was tall and blonde and Captain of the netball team. She was also a terrific bully.

Today, she was at her usual post, standing beneath the lilac tree with a gang of toadies at her feet. They were awful, that lot. The Missing Link, Mel and I called them. Large, stupid and mean. Girls, like Caro, for whom a smile from Deborah or a run up a muddy field in the pouring rain constituted a kind of heaven. They were called Morons. They didn't like us much either.

Then Deborah said, " I promise you, it's true. Ask Sally." And all the Morons turned round and stared at me as if I was something in the zoo. It was very disconcerting. But I wasn't going to let her think she frightened me. (Except she did. She terrified me.) Anyway, I marched up to her and, although my legs were shaking because Caro could certainly have killed me if she'd had a mind, I said , "Ask me what, Deborah?" as if nothing were amiss and we were the best of friends. What an actress! I was lost on those cymbals. I was just hoping she wouldn't tell her Dad to use a blunt needle on me when it was time for my next polio jab.

" Tell them, Sally," announced Her Majesty. I felt like dropping a curtsey. The trouble with Deborah was that she was so grand, she didn't actually speak in sentences like other human beings, so you never knew what she was on about. " Weren't you listening?" She really was the absolute limit. How could I have been at the other end of the playground?

She watched me struggle for a minute and then decided to enlighten me. " You know. How you make babies." She made it sound like a sponge cake. Then she spoke very slowly and kindly the way her Dad did to his patients. " The man puts his willy in your bum and pees."

Caro looked as if she was going to pass out. I hoped she would. It would be like watching a giant oak fall. Timber! She'd probably make a hole in the playground and carry on down to Australia. She went bright red and then a pasty sort of white. I kept my eyes on her. This looked promising.

Katy Fisher was shaken rigid. She turned to Mel. "Do you think your parents do that?"

Mel shrugged, " Bound to." That shook me. Old Mel was full of surprises. All of a sudden, she seemed more interesting.

Then the penny dropped. " My mother doesn't do that!"

Deborah sighed. " She doesn't have to. Your father does it." I shut up then. I wasn't too sure about him.

" Anyway, you've got older sisters, Sally. You know all about this." She had me there. I was about to point out that one of them was barely fourteen and the other was probably insane, when I realised it was in my best interests to pall up with Deborah. Coventry could be a thing of the past, if I played this right. I might even get to be her sort of prime minister. I tried to look superior and a bit bored.

" Course I do. Dr White's and all that." Deborah nodded approvingly. The others looked blank. To tell you the truth, I did know what they were because Mum kept boxes of them in the bathroom cabinet, but I didn't actually know what they were for.

I knew that you got something called the " curse" once a month, and it hurt and Mum made you cinnamon toast and a hot water bottle, but I didn't actually know why. When I used to ask her she would just look grim and say, " You'll find out soon enough, Sally. Never fear." But I wasn't a complete mut. There had to be a reason for it. You couldn't go through all that month after month for nothing. But I knew which side my bread was buttered on. So I smiled knowingly at Deborah Rees Jones and to my delight, she smiled knowingly back. Coventry was over. But it did all sound a bit awful. I was beginning to wonder if having a man was worth it.

94

* * * * * *

Julie came back that evening. She was very quiet. She didn't want to talk to anyone. Not any of us anyhow. She spent most of the evening on the phone. But not to David. I knew that because when it was our turn to clear up after supper - she washed, I wiped - and I asked her. " David okay?" as if it were the most ordinary thing in the world. She just looked straight ahead and said, " David's over, Sally. Ancient history."

She was trying to sound very resolute and certain, but she can't have been that certain because her hands were shaking. She wouldn't speak to me at all after that.

She finished the washing up without looking at me, with the sort of po-faced expression Mel puts on when we are playing Mary, Queen of Scots at Fotheringay. The execution scene. She always wants to be the Queen, but I don't mind because when she looks like that I quite like being the executioner.

I spent all night lying awake, worrying about David. I kept seeing him - the way he sat all huddled up when he cried, his silly grin when he gave me Mrs Fishers' tulip and the way he looked when he saw Julie coming down the road towards him. He really was very nice, even if he did have peculiar hair. He was the first boy ever to be my friend and he was the only man other than Dad and Mum's slimy brother, Andrew, who had ever kissed me. That made him special. That was why I worried about him.

The next morning I watched him go to the tennis club to meet Julie. Except she wasn't there, she was right beside me in her bedroom, trying out a new hairstyle. She was making an awful hash of it. It was called a French pleat and her hair wasn't long enough. So either she scraped it all back so tight it made her look Chinese or it all fell down in big clumps. She can't have been trying because glamour was her thing. Usually, she was good at it. But this morning, her heart wasn't in it.

I was staring out of the window. " He's going to meet you."

" No, he's not." She yanked her hair back as if she wanted to rip it out.

" He'll be waiting."

" Let him." Her eyes looked all glittery and angry.

" He only didn't tell you because he didn't know where to start. It comes from being railroaded."

What are you talking about?"

" Him. David. He told me." Well, he almost had.

" He told you and not me? About the baby?" It was hopeless. Whatever you said just made it worse.

" No. Not exactly."

" Then what exactly? What did he tell you?" She got up and put her shoes on. They were pink but they were pumps. Very flat. Not a good sign.

" He told me that sometimes when you're grown up, you let other people railroad you. You know, make decisions for you. And it's always a disaster. It never works out."

" He said that?"

" Yes." She didn't say anything else. But her eyes were sad and not glittery anymore.

That morning on the bus, Mel and I made our plans. I would break out of school and go and see David and she would tell any teacher who asked that I had an upset and was in the loo. As long as I didn't take too long and clutched my stomach and groaned in the following lesson, we might just get away with it. The only snag was the prefects. They were allowed out in the breaks and if one of them caught me, I was dead.

So I sneaked out at breaktime, crouching down and running along the school wall so that it would hide me. Then past the gates and I was free. I pretended to be Nathanial from " The Last of the Mohicans," escaping from Colonel Monroe. Nathanial was the only white man who could run like a deer and track like Hiawatha. It felt very peculiar to be walking down the

96

street in school uniform during school hours. I hadn't got my hat on either so that was another thing I would be slammed for if I was caught. You weren't supposed to go out without your hat. Actually, you weren't supposed to go out at all until they let you out. It was just like prison really.

Anyway, I got to Harris, Lambert & Iverson without being seen. So I asked the creature at the desk for David and I told her it was a matter of life and death, because I wanted her to hurry. Then I hid behind the plant and ducked down so that no-one could see me through the window. David came running down the stairs straight away. He looked round and couldn't see me. Honestly, he was hopeless. He didn't stand a chance against Lockheart. I crawled out.

" It's me. Over here." I had to whisper. It was part of the secret agent thing.

A Sally, are you okay?"

I didn't have time for him to be stupid. " Look, if anyone catches me, I'm dead. I'm not supposed to be here. I'm not supposed to be anywhere except in the playground. If they find out I'm not in the loo..." And I drew my finger across my throat and pointed to the window.

At last he twigged. He took me through into the corridor where no-one could see us.

" Do you want to see Julie again or don't you?"

" More than anything. I'm dying here, Sall." He was, too. He looked even worse than she did. Sort of pale and a bit grey with deep purple rings around his eyes.

" Then you'll have to do something. Make a big gesture. She needs to know you really love her. More than anyone else in the world. More than your life." I had worked it all out. I had plundered Mum's collection of magazines that she kept in the drawer of her bedside table. They were all about Romance and had articles called things like, " Heartbreak " and " The Course of True Love". I'd spent most of last night pouring over them instead of watching " Bonanza" and I reckoned I'd cracked it.

" What do you want me to do Sall? Kill myself? "

97

If he went on a killing spree everyone in Kenton would be dead and in the Sunday papers.

" Don't be so silly." I'd never spoken to a grown up like that before. It felt wonderful. " Sweep her off her feet." He looked blank. Honestly, it was like breaking rocks. With your head.

"You know, like Simon Templar does. Turn up when she least expects it. Shower her with roses - red ones or diamonds or ....something" I couldn't do it all for him. He was going to have to come up with something. He still looked as if he didn't understood a word. I tried to explain.

" My Dad once bought Mum a mink stole because they had a really bad row and he made her cry." There, that should do it. Show him that we went in for extravagant gestures in our family.

"Mum said he shouldn't have, but she loved it. She kept taking it out of its' box and trying it on in front of the mirror. She cried again then, too. We cry a lot in our family. Take no notice. Just do something wonderful."

I really had to go. If I got back after break was over, I was well and truly sunk. He still looked a bit glum. Perhaps he couldn't afford a mink, what with having to buy a washing machine for Jeannie.

"You could always get her a box of Black Magic instead. She likes those." And that was truly unselfish of me because I hate them. I prefer Milk Tray. He still looked like a dead duck in a thunderstorm. So I gave him a hug and told him to pull himself together. To get it right because I had RISKED EVERYTHING for both of them. He hugged me back a bit then. He really was very sweet. Just a bit gormless.

I ran back to school like the wind, slipped down by the wall and slowly inched my way back into the playground. Good, it was still break. Nothing had changed. Karen was still skipping, Janice was showing everyone her embroidery and Vivian Wolf was sitting on the wall doing other people's homework for sixpence a go.

Then Deborah saw me. She would. But I winked at her and put my hands to my lips. She nodded. Provided I told her what I was up to, she wouldn't tell on me. It wasn't her style. She'd save it up for blackmail purposes later. She'd better watch out, that girl. She'd probably end up running the Mafia and her parents would die of shame. " Doctor's daughter in gangland scandal" - you could see the headlines. Then the bell rang and we all lined up. I'd have to think of something to tell her. Not the truth. She'd never believe me.

* * * * * *

By the time I got home I was feeling pretty pleased with myself. We checked on Julie at Heggarty's, but we didn't stay. Julie wasn't very talkative, anyway. She looked miserable, but I didn't let it bother me. I knew it was only temporary because I had given David the solution. And I had sneaked out of school and got away with it. I really was becoming a Super Sleuth.

I wondered if someone would want to make a TV show about me. Then I could start my Hollywood career playing myself. Which would be a lot easier than playing someone else because I know all about me. On the other hand, I wasn't sure I wanted everyone else to. That might be too much of a good thing. Still, it was a very good start. And I was out of Coventry and on my way to becoming an equal of Deborahs'.

I went up to her after lunch and told her that I had gone out because I had to see a man on urgent business. About the facts of life. You could tell she was impressed, because she didn't hit me. She just nodded at me as if she quite understood, which was more than I did. So I seemed to have got away with that one too.

At home the paragon business was beginning to get me down and I still had another five days to go. I knew my mettle

99

would be tested tonight because Aunty Katy was coming to dinner. In the dining room. Three courses with napkins and manners patrol on red alert. She was already there when I got home because when she came to dinner Mum had to collect her in the afternoon so that she could have a rest and brace herself for the ordeal ahead. It was going to be a very long evening. I had asked if Mel could come too, to help me stand it, and usually she was allowed, but not tonight. The absolute paragon edict was in full force. Which meant no outside help. That was cheating, apparently. So if I was ever going to get any pocket money again, I had to behave. Tricky.

When I got in Aunty Katy was up from her nap and sitting at the kitchen table being fed tea and Fullers' Walnut cake. I asked if I could have some. Very politely and with all the please and " may I" business, but Aunty Katy said no, it was far too rich for a child, so Mum had to make me a piece of toast. Then I had to sit down and eat it with them. I wasn't allowed to take it out into the garden.

A Walk around eating? Whatever next! Sit down, child, and chew your food properly. You'll get tummy ache." I already had because I was cramming the toast in as fast as I could so that I could get away. I swallowed hard and it went down in a big lump that hurt my chest. I drank some water, but it still hurt. I was trying to get escape when Mum stopped me.

" Oh Sally, by the way, I don't want you going to the park. At least, not for the time being." I was horrified. We always went to the park. We'd been going there on our own for years.

" Why not?"

" Don't speak to your mother like that! Parks are nasty places. Full of riffraff."

" Well, there's a particular kind of riffraff I want her to avoid." Mum was raising her eyebrows and looking pointedly at Aunty Katy, so clearly there was something she wanted Aunty Katy to know but not me.

" Susan, why are you pulling faces at me?" Aunty Katy

could be really thick. Mum sighed. Sometimes, Aunty Katy was too much, even for her.

" Because, Aunty," she began patiently, " Mrs Fisher told me there's a man, hanging about in the park". Probably David. They'd hate him, with his floppy hair and pointy shoes. " So I don't want you going there. Do you understand me, Sally?"

I nodded. I understood all right. I just had no intention of obeying her. I went outside, smiling sweetly at both of them. To the garden and Freedom. Making a mental note to ask Mel if her Mum had said anything. Then we could go to the park and investigate.

But first, there was tonight to get through. In due course, Maggie came home and then later Julie and finally Dad. He was always late on days when Aunty Katy was coming to dinner. Then I was hauled in to wash my hands and brush my hair before dinner. Dinner was in the dining room, of course, where everything you saw or touched had belonged either to Aunty Katy's sister (our grandmother) or her mother and was a sort of blessed relic with a full history attached. One she told you about every time she went in there.

"Oh, how well I remember the day when my dear mother/ father/sister/brother/ any old relative at all bought/used/ was given that ..." and she would go off into a sort of orgy of remembering. We must have had the most boring family on earth - because each story went on forever with endless detail but no point, and Dad would go into a sitting up coma and Maggie's eyes would glaze over and Julie would go to the loo and be gone for ages. Only Mum actually listened. She even seemed to like it. Weird.

I lasted out pretty well during the meal. I even managed to slurp my soup without a court martial because Aunty Katy did too. Mum glared at me, but she didn't say anything. Then Julie came back from the loo, which was a mistake because Aunty Katy didn't like her. I don't know why because she was always really nice to her, for Mum's sake, but Aunty Katy asked her if she had given up "prancing around in tights, showing off

101

for a living". Which was really rude. Dad looked about to blow so Mum stepped in, "We think it's wonderful, Aunty. Like being a ballet dancer - only on ice - much more difficult."

Aunty Katy made the kind of noise in her throat that the bathroom pipes do before Dad hits them. "Circus act, more like. You shouldn't encourage her, Susan, to make a spectacle of herself. Most unladylike." Then she resumed slurping her soup.

She always made her feelings very plain, Aunty Katy. She called it honesty being the best policy. But if we'd done it, she'd have called it being impertinent. She wasn't nice to any of us. Not even Mum. Which was odd because Mum was the only person in the universe who bothered about her. The others had all given up because she was so horrible. That was why we always had to put up with her for birthdays and Christmases. Julie called her " the blight".

The only person in the world that Aunty Katy loved was Maggie. Maggie could get away with murder. She always left dinner early claiming she had a vital piece of homework to do, and Aunty Katy would beam and gush and save all her venom for Julie and me. This was because Aunty Katy's father and one of her brothers had been doctors. So she felt that Maggie was upholding the family tradition.

She would pat Maggie's hand (she never patted my hand. I had to kiss her whiskery old cheek). She had hands like an old oak root - bumpy and gnarled with sticking out veins. Not very clean. She had a lot of rings. All left to her by her dead relatives. She had a big diamond ring that was lovely. It sparkled and shone and you could see all different coloured lights in it. But there was no point in admiring it. It was for the medical profession only. The day Maggie qualified it was to be handed over to her. I once wondered what would happen if Aunty Katy popped her clogs before that day arrived, because she was very old and Maggie was only fourteen and still had a way to go yet. I asked Dad and he smiled a sort of tight smile and said " Oh, it probably reverts to the BMA, Sally." I didn't know what that was, but you could tell he didn't approve. He thought Mum

102

should get it. We all did.

In the meantime, Mum and Julie cleared the soup and went to get the roast for Dad to carve, and the good news was that Aunty Katy was beginning to nod off. She didn't have much stamina in the dining stakes. She probably would have rather had something on a tray in front of the TV. She was always falling asleep in the middle of things. She couldn't help it. It was because she was so old. She fell asleep at the dining table one Christmas and nearly fell into her mince pie and custard, but Mum fished her out just in time. We laughed and laughed, all three of us. I thought I was going to be sick, I laughed so much. But Mum got cross and said that Dad had given her too much wine. He said that was rubbish because she had hollow legs, so perhaps that was why she wore those bandages. Then he helped Mum carry her into the sitting room and lay her down on the sofa and she snored all the way through the Queens' Speech. It was brilliant. Better than a show.

No such luck tonight. Mum said, "Wake up, Aunty, you'll miss your dinner," a bit sharply because she was cross about what she had said about Julie. And Aunty Katy's head jerked up and she looked round as if she didn't know us, like an old tortoise poking it's head out of it's shell after the winter and not liking what it saw. She was in a bad mood for the rest of the meal. Poor old Mum couldn't get anything right. The meat was too tough, the beans weren't properly cooked, and she should never make her apple pie like that because it made the pastry soggy.

Mum was nearly in tears. She went all red and said less and less as the evening went on. And it did go on. For ages. I knew she'd upset Mum because Dad started saying how lovely the meal was, just how he liked it, in a loud voice. You could tell he felt really sorry for her. Then he ran away to his study. He always said he had work to do when Aunty Katie came, but once when I took his coffee in, he wasn't working at all. He was reading the paper. He winked at me on the way out, so I knew the paragon business was going well. I made an extra effort to help and carried everything out for Mum, not dropping a single fork. And she thanked me and said I was a sweetie, and just to stack it all up in the sink and she'd do it later. But Julie said, no, Mum had done all the cooking and she and I would do it together when Mum was driving Aunty Katy home. And Mum hugged us both and said we were good girls. So that was a turnup for the books! I would have to make an appointment with Dad in the study to bring the pocket money review forward.

Julie and I ran the water for the washing up and I started a bubble fight with the Fairy liquid to cheer her up. It seemed to be working when Aunty Katy came in to say goodbye. We didn't notice her at first, we were too busy yelling and throwing handfuls of foam at each other. She just stood in the doorway and watched us. She didn't say anything.

When we realised she was there, we shut up. Julie put the bottle down and wiped the froth off her clothes. Then she wiped the froth moustache and beard off my face.

We thought we'd be for it, but Aunty Katy just looked at us and said very quietly, " Lovely to be young. Lovely to have a sister." And then she turned and walked away.

And we felt sorry for her. Because everybody she had loved was dead.

CHAPTER 10

The big gesture wasn't long in coming. David might have been slow on the up take, but once he'd got it, he went for broke.

The next morning very, very early a huge bouquet of roses was left at the back door. Red roses. Hundreds of them. For Julie. There was a small package wrapped in silver paper hidden among the flowers with her name on it. The roses were beautiful - deep, dark red and velvety. Dad found them when he unlocked the back door and put the milk bottles out. "Julie, you've got an admirer!" He shouted out and we all came racing down in our nighties to see. Even Maggie.

Mum examined them carefully. She was the bouquet expert in our family. Well, she was the only one who ever got them -until now- and then only on anniversaries and very special occasions.

"Oh, Julie, they're long-stemmed ..." You could tell from her tone of voice that was good. She bent over to sniff them to see if the scent came up to scratch and exclaimed, A Look! There are nineteen of them. One for every year of your life. What a lovely gesture! Who are they from, dear?"

Julie just stood there in her baby dolls. But you could tell she was pleased. She liked grand gestures. That was because she was a theatrical. And this was all because of me. I couldn't stop grinning. My plan had worked a treat. At last!

Mum stood back and graciously allowed us to look at the flowers as if they were something in a museum. Julie immediately spotted the package. She took it out of the flowers and walked away to open it on her own.

"Well! I'll be damned..." Dad sat down and poured Mum a cup of tea. Normally, he took it upstairs to her. Mum ran cold water into the sink and put the flowers in it.

"Who can they be from?" Mum was all a twitter. She loved this kind of thing. Romance, you see, like the mags she kept hidden in her bedroom drawer.

"Someone who means business, Suzy. Roses like that cost a fortune." Dad knew what he was on about because twice a year he bought them for Mum. On her birthday and their anniversary. But never so many as this. Not in one go.

"Who do you think it could be?" Mum was like a broken record. Her brain was stuck in one groove.

"Haven't a clue. Ask Sally."

Thank you, Miss Maggie Palmer. I knew she'd get me for the rosebush. Just when I was feeling so happy. Now, as they all turned to stare at me, swivelling round like a battery of guns, I felt like a burst balloon.

"How should I know?" I hoped that would convince them.

"Do you know who they're from?" It was quite difficult to actually lie to Dad. He tended to spot it. Whereas Mum would believe almost anything, if you got your story right. I looked down and hoped I wasn't going red.

"Ah, no. I don't. Actually. Er..." I had to be careful not to meet his eye.

"I've got to go now because I'm meeting Mel early. We've got a test." Whew!

"You're not leaving this house, Sally, until you've washed and eaten your breakfast. No sneaking out when I'm not looking. Do I make myself clear?"

Mum was back on form. I raced upstairs to Julie's room. The door was locked. I rapped on it with my hand.

"It's me. Open the door."

Maggie was watching from the top of the stairs.

"Nice try, Sall. You may fool them, but you don't fool me. You can tell me later." And she turned and walked down the corridor to her room. I pulled a face, wishing she'd keep her mind on her dead frogs and not keep trying to dissect me.

Julie unlocked the door and let me in. She was holding a box. The silver wrapping paper lay in a crumpled heap on the bed. There was a folded piece of paper on her dressing table.

"What did he say?" This was no time for faffing around. I had to know. She held up the green leather box. It looked expensive.

"What's in it?"

"You're awful, Nosey Parker. No privacy with you around." But she was smiling and she opened the box. Something inside caught the light and sent a tiny rainbow across the carpet. It was a ring. A diamond ring. It wasn't big like Aunty Katy's, but it was much prettier. Three little diamonds all twisted round in a little loop. Like half a bow.

"It's a lovers' knot." Julie explained and she took it out for me to see.

"It's...beautiful." I whispered it because David had so fulfilled my dreams for them, I was overwhelmed. I felt very quiet and solemn and a bit carried away. Like being in church on Christmas Eve. You know, you walk in out of a dark, cold night, probably raining, and suddenly there it all is. Christmas. Candles and music and Baby Jesus in the manger. And for a minute it sort of takes your breath away. Even if you know he's only a doll.

David had done it all. Flowers, a ring and a letter too. All tokens of his love. It was perfect. Better even than Dad's mink because to go from nothing to all this was ...well, superb!

She held the ring out in the palm of her hand for me to see. I picked it up and looked at it, turning it round so that it caught the light.

"Put it on." She shook her head.

"Why not?" Crikey, what was wrong with her ?

"Because he has to do that. Because he says it's not just a ring, it's a promise." She was smiling so hard, her jaw must have ached.

"What did he say in the note?"

Julie laughed. "Sally, you are the nosiest old Parker in

107

the whole wide world."

I was in agony here! I had to know. I was dying to know! I deserved to know, because I had risked everything to put him straight. Couldn't she tell it was all because of me? I must have looked a bit tormented because she picked the note up and began to read.

"To the most beautiful girl in the world, my lovely Julie. You are the love of my life. I want to be with you forever." Blimey, that was telling her!

"Go on. Don't stop." I wanted to hear the rest. But her voice was going a bit crackely and she shook her head and wouldn't go on. I walked over to the window. I was staggered. He had got it so right. I hadn't expected this. To tell you the truth, I hoped he would hit the jackpot with the present because he wasn't so hot with the words. But this ... this was almost poetry. I needn't have worried at all. It was as good as anything in any of Mum's magazines. For a minute, I wondered if he'd bought one. You know, cribbed a bit. Julie folded up the note.

"There's more. A lot more. But it's private, Madam Parker." And she gave me a huge hug as if she was practising for him. "I must rush now because I need to talk to David," and she bundled me out of the room. My ribs were broken, but I was grinning like she was now. I couldn't help it.

She was happy again. I knew it. She had that kind of glow back and it was all because of me. And he would be happy too. No more tears! I had fixed it. Perhaps I would end up in the U.N., fixing the world. When I was very old, thirty or something, and my Hollywood days were over. You have to think of the future.

Then I remembered Jeannie. If all went well for Julie, she wouldn't have much of a future. She wouldn't be happy either, because she loved David. You could tell by the look on her face when she talked about him. I bet she didn't know about the flowers or the ring. Or even about Julie. That worried me.

But then I cheered up because Jeannie would have the baby and she had said herself that that was all she'd ever wanted, so perhaps it would be enough. I hoped so anyway.

Maybe one of David's pals in the Mafia would take her on. She wasn't pretty like Julie, but she wasn't that bad, and he could look after them, like Joseph did with Mary and Jesus. Jesus wasn't his child either. That worked out all right.

As I walked back to my room I could hear Julie opening and closing drawers and humming a little tune. So everything was fine, at last. And I had saved her and stuck us all back together, like Mum said you should in times of trouble.

I was so pleased I got dressed in record time and was downstairs even before Dad left

"This is an unprecedented honour, Sally." It was a bit sarcastic, but he was like Mags, he couldn't help it. He buttered me a piece of toast and passed me my best jam, not the sour old marmalade with bits in that he always has. That was horrible. Mum was still smiling and pouring more tea for him, so you could tell she was in a good mood.

I beamed at them both. "It's a very good day." I announced. Mum winked at me and drank some of her tea.

"You're very cheerful for someone who's got a test coming up. Why is that?" Dad was smiling when he said it, so I knew he was teasing.

"Because of the flowers, of course."

"Ah Susan, if she carries on like this when someone sends her sister flowers, whatever will she be like when she gets some of her own?"

"She'll get lots of flowers when she's grown up. And so will Maggie." Mum was very loyal.

"I think they're lovely." They were. Their scent filled the whole room.

"So they are, sweetie, so they are." Mum was on cloud nine and she wasn't coming down. She liked a world that was full of Romance, so I had helped her too. Dad groaned.

"Oh lord, three Romantics in the family! Thank God for Maggie, that's all I can say." And I wondered for a moment if he were a teeny bit jealous. Because, until this morning, Dad and his mink and anniversary flowers were the only romantic gestures we had in this family. He stood up and bent down to kiss Mum goodbye.

"Got to go. Have a good day, you two." And then he went off to work.

Julie rushed out of the house without arranging the roses. Mum did that. They took three vases. Two went in Julie's room and the other one we snitched for the sitting room. Julie didn't mind. She had so many. They were glorious.

She raced off to see David. She'd made a special effort. No French pleat or flat shoes today. She wore her red sandals and a thin white dress with a halter neck and a soft, floaty skirt. Her shoulders were bare. She was quite brown already, so it looked very nice. She got brown very quickly. Like Dad. She never went through the bright red and burned stage, she just cut to the chase and went a sort of peachy brown straight away. Typical.

I took one of the vases upstairs for Mum, while she was still arranging the sitting room one, and watched out of the window as Julie flew down the street and straight into David's arms. Right there on the street corner. They hugged and kissed as if they would never stop. They didn't seem to care if anyone could see them now. They both knew they had nearly lost the most important thing in their lives and they weren't going to let it go ever again. You could tell. They were serious now. The smooch went on for so long I felt a bit embarrassed watching, but not too much because I was a secret agent after all and you have to be prepared for these things. Anyway, it was good for picking up tips. You can't afford to be too squeamish about that, either. So I kept watching. In the end, they walked away towards the club, holding hands. But things were different now. You could tell. They meant business.

* * * * *

It got hotter and hotter. The flowers in the gardens wilted and the grass in the playing field went brown. We were in the final stages of rehearsals for the school play. It was very hot sitting all cooped up in the hall with the rest of the band. We had to sit stock still and not breathe a word. It was very boring because Mel was right. The play was awful when you had to watch it. I hadn't noticed before because I was too busy acting, but it was a really silly subject to start with - a sort of mishmash of Dick Whittington with Good Queen Bess (Miss Travess - the elecution teacher - in a red nylon wig) thrown in.

Mel said it was rubbish historically. It was very badly performed. Janet Elkins, who played the lead because she had long, blonde hair, couldn't remember her words and tended to burst into tears in the middle of a scene or ask Miss Roberts what came next. Elizabeth Earle still couldn't tell left from right and crashed into Angela Humber now, instead of me. No murders or shipwrecks, nobody risking life or death for the love of anyone, no good songs, it was chronic. And if you were stuck in the band with only one crash on the cymbals in the whole thing, then it was actually quite difficult to stay awake. I kept nodding off in the middle of everything. Just like Aunty Katy. Depressing, really.

Mum and Dad were going away. It was Dad's annual conference. He went every year for four days and Mum would go down for the Dinner and Dance on the last day and drive him back. He always went down on the train. This year it was in Eastbourne. Mum had said she wouldn't go this time, she would stay and see me be the Third Gypsy. But when I was demoted to the cymbals, they asked if I minded if she went after all. I had to say no because it was a bit much to miss a Dinner and Dance in Eastbourne for one bash on the cymbals.

So I told her she should go. But then I felt a bit ...well, abandoned, sort of. Mum always came to see me in everything. Dad came sometimes, but Mum always. Ever since I was a

Butterfly in the kindergarten ballet, Mum had sat through everything I had ever done and told me it was wonderful, even when it wasn't. So, although I pretended to be very grown up and said I didn't mind at all, actually I did because she was my Mum and her place was with me, really. But they both looked very pleased and said this being so good was part of my being a paragon, the last part, and that pocket money would be resumed on Saturday as usual. So I'd only lost one week. And when I said I thought I would ask Julie to come instead, Mum beamed and said she'd always hoped we girls would stick together so we'd never be alone and now, after all the fighting, we were. So she was really pleased.

When I asked Julie if she would come, otherwise I'd be the only person who had no-one there, she said of course she would, when was it and she'd take the afternoon off. I think Mum must have primed her first, because she didn't seem at all surprised and said there'd be no problem because Mr Heggarty always let her do what she wanted. So I told her that was good because at least I'd have the most glamorous sister there, so I'd stand out for something. Then she asked me if I wanted her to make me up for the play, but I had to say no because I thought Miss Roberts would go into orbit if I turned up with green eyelids and orange nails. I was tempted though. Even if she put me in detention forever, it might have been worth it.

The morning of the play Mum laid her evening dress across the back seat of her car in a cellophane bag and set off for Eastbourne. She went early because she had a long drive ahead of her.

It was hotter than ever. There was no breeze at all and the class room was stuffy and airless. Everyone was hot and sticky and bad-tempered. Julia Ambrose smelled. No-one wanted to sit next to her because of danger of asphyxiation. Our hair stuck to our foreheads and we were all sweaty. Even Deborah Rees Jones had a shiny nose.

We ran through the play all morning and then went into lunch. Nobody wanted to eat, but Miss Steed, our school

112

matron, gave us no quarter. Her father had been a general or something in the army, so she wore a green overall, stood up straight and expected us to eat tapioca pudding in all weathers. She said faddy eating was where the rot started. Apparently, she had eaten hot tapioca pudding in Africa all the time in the burning sun and that was what had made the British Empire great. (If it didn't kill you first.) She had to be joking. Surely you couldn't conquer a continent with a hot pudding? Perhaps they made the poor old Africans eat it and they all dropped dead. You could see why. Especially if you weren't used to it. It was bad enough if you were.

Anyway, I pushed this awful white slime around my plate with the spoon and I just couldn't eat it. So Miss Steed screamed at me and told me I had no backbone and she didn't know what the world was coming to.

Then we filed into the hall and got ready for the play. It was baking in there because the windows were very small and high up, and all the air they let in was up there in the ceiling, so you couldn't breathe it down where we were. The band had to go in first and sit on benches in front of the stage. We sat there for ages while the others got ready. Then the Mums and Dads started to arrive and I started to panic. Julie wasn't there.

What if she didn't come? What if she had forgotten? What if Mr Heggarty had decided not to give her the afternoon off or David had ran amok and killed Jeannie and the Battleaxe? It could happen. In this heat. Then I'd have no-one to come to the play. Mel's Mum and Dad arrived and gave me a cheery wave. That made me feel even worse. And it was so hot the Mums fanned themselves with their programmes and some of the Dads took their jackets off. I wished mine were there. The hall was almost full now and still no Julie. My eyes felt all prickly. I hoped I wouldn't cry because I was sitting next to Deborah Rees Jones and you could bet your life that if I blubbed, she'd laugh and then I'd hit her and be back in Coventry or worse. I might even be expelled. Miss Roberts rustled her music and sat down at the piano. Then she coughed

113

and that was the sign we were about to begin.

As if on cue, because she was a better actress than anyone in that hall, Julie walked in. Slowly she walked down the aisle to the front row, just behind me. Everyone turned and gawped at her. She looked fabulous. Like a real film star. She had pulled ALL the stops out. She wore a tight black dress that made her walk funny and Mum's mink stole that she hadn't taken with her because it was too hot. Mum would have killed her.

Her make up and hair were perfect. Bright, glossy lips, huge black-rimmed eyes and soft curly hair. She took forever to walk down that aisle and when she sat down, she blew me a kiss. I nearly stood up and cheered.

Everyone was looking at her. The Mums looked a bit fed up and the Dads couldn't take their eyes off her. They kept smiling that silly smile that men do when they think someone's sexy. The one that makes them look a bit daft. Some of them handed her their programmes. By the time she sat down, she had five.

The Mums were all wearing flowery dresses in pink or blue. They looked sort of faded beside Julie. She always did that. Looked more than everyone else. More colourful, more pretty, more sexy. She was just more of everything, really.

And I felt very pleased with her because she had made an effort and done me proud. And she wasn't alone. She had brought David with her. He had made an effort, too. He wore a grey suit with a blue tie and normal shoes. His hair was still peculiar, but you can't have everything. I nudged Deborah in the ribs and whispered: "That's the man who kissed me. He's taken the afternoon off work." Her jaw dropped and she forgot to come in on the flute with Miss Roberts, who was playing the opening bars. She had to play them again twice before Deborah recovered. It was wonderful. Nobody looked at the play. They were all too busy looking at Julie. And I was a celebrity. Because she was mine. They both were.

* * * * *

After the show everyone crowded round Julie. All the kids, that is. They had all seen her in the ice show last Christmas. It was brilliant. People who never wanted to even look at me, let alone speak to me, suddenly discovered we were best friends. They were such creeps. Karen Oakley, who was the prettiest girl in the class, came up to me and tried to hold my hand! We had hated each other ever since Kindergarten, when she played the angel Gabriel in the nativity play and I was so cross at only being a Shepherd that I pushed her off the cloud she was standing on. She fell over and her dress tore, well, it was her mother's nightie actually, and you could see her knickers. You're not supposed to see an angels' knickers. Everyone laughed and she never forgave me. Now, she told me she realised that "we've been friends since we were babies, so we were practically family!" Oh! and could she meet Julie? Perhaps she thought she was her family too. You had to hand it to her. For sheer cheek she took the cake.

Then Caro came up to me and made my day. She asked me if I would introduce her to Julie. "Not a chance, Caro, she only speaks to humans. And she doesn't like people who thump her sister, either. So I wouldn't do that again if I were you, on account of the fact that her boyfriend, the one over there in the grey suit, is in the Mafia, so if you don't want to end up dead in a ditch, better be nice to me from now on."

That settled her hash. It was a very good moment. Then Julie told me to get my things so that we could go home. She'd had enough of moron adoration.

When I was getting my blazer, Deborah asked me if she could say hello to Julie and tell her how much she'd loved her as the Ice Queen in the Wembley show. That was different. First of all, she was Deborah and could make my life hell, and secondly, she had actually bothered to remember what Julie had done in

115

the show. So that was more like it. I took her up to Julie and she gushed all over her. Julie just let her grovel and didn't say a word. Then Deborah's Mum came up to drag her away before she made a complete spectacle of herself. Julie had that effect on people. She could reduce them to gibbering wrecks. Usually men. David was laughing his head off.

Julie smiled at Deborah and said sweetly, "You're the doctors' daughter, aren't you?" And Deborah puffed up and said "Yes". Then Julie smiled angelically at Deborah's Mum and said that the doctor was a lovely man, so kind and understanding and so funny, and she must see him again because he was just the best doctor ever. And Deborah's Mum looked a bit worried then because no-one wanted Julie to like their men that much. Or see them very often. So she bustled Deborah away. Julie winked at me. She had done it all deliberately. David had to sit down, he was laughing so much. She could be quite wicked sometimes. But a lot of fun.

Julie and David went home with me on the bus. Julie put Mum's mink away in it's box so that she wouldn't know it had been borrowed and then went out with David before Maggie came home. I had never been alone in the house before. It was only for an hour, but it felt kind of weird. Big and empty. Terribly quiet. I didn't like it.

Then Mags came back and banged the door and dropped her satchel on the kitchen floor and made me a sandwich. So things went back to normal. Almost. Except I did miss Mum. I went into her room and it felt peculiar without her.

Her slippers were under the chair and her dressing gown hung up behind the door. Her things were everywhere, but she wasn't. The room still smelled of her. Blue Grass by Elizabeth Arden. She loved it. Dad always gave her a huge box at Christmas full of talcum powder and bath salts and perfume and soap. All Blue Grass. It was Mum, that smell. She always wore it. The little glass deer I had given her for her birthday was on her dressing table. This room was making me feel sad, so I left it. Julie had said she would bring fish and chips home for supper as a treat. She said we could eat it with our fingers out of the newspaper. Mum never let us do that. So, Julie was making a real effort to be good to us while Mum was away. But I still felt sad without her. She always nagged about elbows and knives and forks, but it was better when she was there.

I decided to have a bath. A big, deep one with lots of bubbles to practise for Hollywood. They always have baths like that there. I ran the bath and put lots of bubble bath in. Much more than Mum would have let me. It was called Matey and it had pictures of Captain Pugwash on the packet. Bit babyish, but it made very good bubbles. Then I got in and had a think.

I wondered what it would really be like to be grown up. To be like Julie. To be pretty and have men fall in love with you and women be jealous of you. To have bosoms and a figure men wanted to touch. I wished I had all that. I looked down to see if there were any signs of my bosoms hatching out, but nothing. Flat as a pancake. So I lay back and had a bit of a day dream. I day dreamed I was Julie - with high heels and everyone wanting to know me. But David kept coming into the dream. I couldn't get rid of him. Just when I was concentrating on what I would look like - the best of everything - a bit of Natalie Wood with Elizabeth Taylor and Julie thrown in - he would pop up. I couldn't stop him. He looked quite dishy when he dressed normal. Older, more handsome. Less of a goof.

I kicked him out of the dream because he was taken. Then I started to think about the man I would want. I figured Cookie from "Sunset Strip" to have fun with, Simon Templar of course to show off with and Dr Kildare to adore me. But they all kept turning into David. I kept seeing his face when he had smiled at me and told me not to worry about getting a man. The way his eyes creased up when he laughed. He had very nice eyes. Dark and brown and sort of velvety. Then I realised I didn't want Cookie or Simon Templer, or even Dr Kildare. I wanted David. But he was Julies'.

I went on with my think. He wasn't mine, but I had risked everything for him and he had come with Julie to see my play, even though I was only on the cymbals, to stick by me. Because he was a true friend and I loved him. I think he loved me too. Just a little bit. Because I had helped right from the very start and he always talked to me about things. So, although he belonged to Julie, he belonged to me a bit, too.

Downstairs, the phone rang. Maggie must have answered it because it stopped so quickly. Upstairs, my think was making me sad because it was hopeless. I mean, it was bad enough for David and Julie, but for me and him it was a complete non starter. It would take me years to catch up and be old enough and by then he'd be an old man. Almost as old as Dad.

Perhaps Julie wouldn't want him then. Perhaps I wouldn't either.

This think was going round in circles. The water was getting cold too. So I hauled myself out of the bath and looked at my reflection in the mirror. I was covered in white foam. I looked like a Yeti. I lumbered across the frozen wastes of the bathroom floor to get a towel. Then the door opened. It was Maggie.

"All right, who is he?" I wished she wouldn't do that. She always ruined my game.

"Who?" I flicked some foam onto the floor and shaped it into a little mound. Like an igloo.

"You know who. Mystery man. The one the whole school is talking about. The one everybody knows about except me."

She glared at me. "Don't do that. You're making a mess." My lovely igloo was already dissolving into a soapy puddle. Maggie looked fed up. She put the lid down on the toilet and sat on it. She wasn't going to budge until I told her.

I wondered how she knew. Who could have told her? Must have been Annabel - Karen Oakley's sister. She was in Maggie's class. She'd be on the jungle drums as soon as Karen had told her in the car on the way home. She must have rung Maggie. The whole world would know now.

Annabel was the school's public information service.

118

She knew everything about everybody - usually before they did. And she would broadcast it loud and clear. Now she knew about David.

"He's called David Something or other. I can't remember. He used to be at Claremont."

Julie had never gone to Heathwood School for Girls. When she was eleven Dad didn't have the money. That came later when he went into partnership with Mr Miller. So Julie just went to the ordinary high school in Preston Road. That was where she met David and Jeannie.

"Oh. Didn't he marry Jeannie Dodwell?" Maggie didn't have a memory. She had a filing system. And she was older than me. She could remember more.

"Yup. She's going to have a baby."

"Golly. I take it Mum and Dad don't know?"

"No-one knows. I only know because I followed them." I left Mel out. I didn't think Maggie would appreciate strangers knowing while she was still in the dark.

"That figures. Well, it's common knowledge now. It's only a matter of time 'til they find out." She folded her arms and pulled a face. A We know she loves him. Does he love her? Do you think?"

"Yes."

She sighed. "Gets better and better, doesn't it?" Then she looked at me. I was covered in goose bumps. "You'd better dry yourself. Why didn't you tell me before?"

"I promised not to. I crossed my heart."

She nodded again. "Okay. Forget about the rosebush. We're quits now." And she went away.

Maggie never commented on what people did. Or very rarely. That was why she was such a lousy gossip. Because she saw things differently. She didn't see people like Julie and I did. The whole secret world they carry round with them, like a snail with it's shell. The things they love and hate, what they dream of or long for. She just didn't see any of that. What she did see was biology - a series of systems all working together, heart

119

pumping, lungs breathing, blood running around in the veins. And she was very good at understanding that, but the whole mystery of a person didn't exist for her at all. Sometimes, I felt sorry for her. Because she was incredibly fair. Nearly always. Unlike us.

* * * * * *

Now that Maggie knew and Julie and David had thrown caution to the winds, the secret mission fell to bits. We still called into Heggarty's after school every day to try and head off Lockheart, but he wouldn't have had much trouble finding them now, so maybe he wasn't trying. More likely, he was playing a long game. David was probably only small fry in the gangster world and Lockheart must have been after the ring leader.

Perhaps he had a mission to round up the whole gang, and he wanted to do it all at once so he'd get a promotion and be covered in glory. He might even get a medal. From the Queen. Obviously, he was biding his time, so I decided to bide mine too. I'd keep an eye on them, but there wasn't much I could do to protect them now. They saw each other all the time and they walked around holding hands. They didn't seem to care about being secret anymore. I decided to wait and see how things panned out.

Anyway, it would be much easier when school had broken up and we were on holiday. We could be much more flexible then and I wouldn't have to risk being expelled if they needed my protection. Mel and I talked it through and we decided to put our mission on hold until the holidays began. Then we could regroup and see how the land lay. I just prayed I wasn't wrong and Lockheart wouldn't pounce and catch us all napping. I hoped the heat had got him too.

In any case, we didn't have much time for being secret agents because the tennis season began. We hated it.

When Wimbledon started the grown ups went into a frenzy. Perfectly normal Mums and Dads who moaned if they had to walk to the shops and were always far too busy to play in the garden, now put on white shorts and started jumping about the tennis courts. The club was full of them. People you never saw at all for the rest of the year suddenly popped up. Only the diehards played regularly, but in the month surrounding Wimbledon, everyone who had a racquet was on the courts. They were everywhere, like ants. You couldn't get away from them. Even Mum and Dad. I nearly died of shame. Fortunately, they mostly played with each other which limited the embarrassment a bit.

All of us kids were roped in as ball boys or helpers at the tennis teas. We had to hand round the bridge rolls. They were brown and glossy like the toy loaves in my dolls' house kitchen. But they were made of sawdust. They had little flags on them which said salmon or chicken, but you couldn't taste the difference. They sat on lacy paper doillies on Mrs Charlesworth's second best china and you had to make sure they didn't slide off into someone's lap when you handed them round. Mel was pouring out the iced lemonade once and she poured it straight into Mr Reynolds's lap. She didn't notice that he hadn't got a glass. She wasn't concentrating. They took her off the tennis teas. But not me. We had to be polite at all times and we couldn't say no. It was actually slavery.

Being a ball boy was better, even if you were always painting that white stuff on your plimsolls. Mel and I were usually a team because the rules said there had to be two. You had to run around like crazy collecting up all the balls, but at least you got a round of tepid applause and a glass of iced lemonade at the end. There was never anything left for us to eat. Well, there were always bridge rolls leftover, but they were so foul even we wouldn't eat them. The only thing worth eating was Pauline Charlesworth's chocolate cake and that always went

121

first. Because it was very good. They used to have little glass bowls of strawberries and cream, and they were absolute bliss but they stopped that because they said the sugar attracted flies. We thought it was because we always nicked them despite the threats. They were the only eats worth being punished for.

So, for the moment, slavery was on and the park was off. We hadn't seen Tim and Rusty for ages, which was a real shame because they were both so nice and Rusty could actually get the ball which was more than most of the tennis players could.

There was no escape. It went on all weekend and some evenings, too. Match after match. Tennis tournaments, they were called. People came to sit and watch. So the club was out for Julie and David. There wasn't room for them. They started going to the park instead. For a bit of privacy. Some people had all the luck. They had their love and all we had was the tennis teas. Honestly, it made you want to spit.

I was very quiet these days. Everyone remarked on it. At school and at home. They thought it was the heat. It wasn't. After I realised that I loved David, I felt very odd because I knew that he was Julie's. And it was a bit as if part of me was cut off and kept in quarantine, because when I did think about it, it made me miserable. I didn't even tell Mel. I kept it locked up, hidden away. But it felt very peculiar because it was always there.

I could feel it even when I didn't think about it. It was like a lump in my throat. But it was no good. He was never going to love me. He had Julie. Sometimes I wished she'd just go away and leave him to me. But that was very muddling, because my whole mission had been to protect her and now part of what I was protecting her from was me. So I tried not to think about it. But sometimes when I saw him (which was a lot less than before because they were out in the open now and I no longer had to go to Harris, Iverson and Lambert, so I never saw him on my own), and he smiled at me, I really longed for him to hug me again and it gave me a kind of ache because he didn't. Mum's magazines called it heart ache. I know because I read it

122

up.

I tried not to think about it, but it made me sad, secretly, a lot of the time. And I wondered if growing up was such a good idea, because along with the high heels and the bosoms, you also got this and it hurt.

CHAPTER 11

I missed not being a Super sleuth. Now that the mission was on hold I didn't feel important anymore and I didn't like that. Still, I consoled myself with the fact that school was about to break up and then it would be the SUMMER HOLIDAYS, which were the best of all because they went on forever. I talked to Mel and we considered if we could expand our secret agent business to include someone other than Julie. I hoped so because I loved it, even though it had been very worrying. But that was because Julie was my sister and David my true friend, so if it were strangers, I reckoned I wouldn't mind so much. Seeing them get nabbed by Lockheart or gunned down by the Mafia would only be what Dad called "an occupational hazard". We would have plenty of time for sleuthing in the hols. We decided the best place to start our new mission would be the park. Although Mum had tried to ban me, she was only fussing. It all looked very promising.

In the meantime, the heatwave went on. Every morning the sun shone and the sky was blue, but in the afternoon it went pale, the colour sort of bleached out. The streets were dry and dusty and the bus was unbearable on the way home from school. The plush seats were the worst, so we tried to keep standing up because it was cooler, but they wouldn't always let you.

The grass in the verges died and the flowers withered, but not in our garden because of Dad's sprinkler system. Every evening when he came home from work, he turned it on and nothing died.

Rainbow jets of cool water rained down on the plants

and me. Our grass stayed green and the flowers were bright and strong.

I loved the heat as long as I could stay in the garden where there was always shade. I never got tired or suffered from the "heat exhaustion" Mum was always talking about. The only thing I really hated was my school hat. We had to wear these awful panama hats with elastic under the chin. Mine was too small (inherited from Maggie, who, despite all her brains, had a very small head), so the band dug into my forehead and the elastic into my chin, but Mum refused to buy a new one "just for a few weeks". You had to wear it all the way home. Because there were prefects on the bus and if you took it off, they'd kill you. It was torture, honestly. Perhaps they thought if our brains got very hot, we'd get cleverer. Sort of like a greenhouse, but it didn't seem to be working because as the heat went on and the classrooms got hotter and stuffier, we did worse and worse in our tests. We couldn't concentrate. In the end, they even gave up shouting at us. Perhaps they thought we were suffering enough in that getup. Because you had to wear your blazer out of school as well and they were all wool. The label said so. What made matters worse was that while we trudged along in clothes that made us look like proper Charlies, everyone else was dressed as if they were on holiday.

Even the Mums had bare legs now. And people wore shorts in the street. I'd never seen that except at the seaside. I couldn't wait to join them. Julie wore tops that looked like a swimsuit all the time. Halter necks she called them. But she was nice and brown. She never got freckly like Mags and me. Maggie said it was because our skins didn't suit the sun, but she could speak for herself because mine loved it, along with the rest of me. It was just a bit speckled, that's all. Like those dear little eggs that cost more.

Me and my skin would run in and out of the sprinklers every evening and pretend to be Captain Cook in a tropical storm or Clive of India in a monsoon. Often Mel came round to join in. She didn't have sprinklers at home. It was good when

126

Mel came because her knowing all about history gave us alternatives. She could tell me the story and I would make up the play. I was better at that, but she knew a lot of stories so we made a good team. Clive of India was madly in love with a beautiful Indian princess called Julie. The princess was forbidden to see Clive by her cruel tyrant of a father and she wore the most beautiful silken saris all the time. Except in our case it was Mum's old sheet from the ironing board. Or we would run about in our knickers, which was all you wanted to wear in this weather, and pretend we were aboriginal natives, savage princesses who knew the secret of medicinal herbs and how to survive in the tropics. Where to find the best grubs. That sort of thing. Because that was what they ate. Honestly.

In our play we roamed about the world, travelling from shore to shore in our rockery boat, from the South China Seas to the Pacific and the Indian Ocean and on to Africa. Our geography roamed about a bit, too.

I wasn't sure if Captain Cook ever went to China or Clive of India to the Pacific, but they did with us. We let them roam about everywhere. And always one of us was a princess of some sort or another. We took it in turns. We were very fond of being princesses. I don't know why because they always had such horrible families, wicked fathers who locked them up so they had to escape into the arms of their one true love. Usually poor old Clive of India because Captain Cook was a bit tied up with the discovering. We played these games for hours. And they let us because it was the only way to stay cool and it was almost the end of term anyway, so homework was a lost cause.

Supper was always cold now because of not wanting to put the oven on in this heat. So if you were late, they moaned a bit, but it didn't really matter.

Julie stayed out until very late now. She didn't even pretend to come home for supper. She still hadn't told Mum the truth, but it couldn't be long before Mum found out because Maggie had said that if Mum ever asked her directly she wouldn't lie. She wouldn't volunteer the information, either, she said, but if questioned, she wouldn't lie. She wasn't very big on secrets, Maggie. Julie just used to tell Mum she was out with a friend and Mum didn't interrogate her because she was nearly grown-up. But you could tell that Mum was puzzled that Julie didn't tell her more because up to now Julie had always told her everything. She used to frown a bit when Julie breezed in when the news was on and airily announce she'd been out with a friend. Without saying who. But Mum didn't make anything of it.

Perhaps she was biding her time too. And Dad never noticed anything when the evening news was on. That was sacred in our house. We could have all been butchered by a band of brigands and he wouldn't have batted an eyelid. Not if it happened during the Nine O'Clock News.

Julie bought two electric fans back from Heggartys for us.They were all he had left. The rest were sold out. She gave one to Mum and Dad and kept one for herself. But when it was very hot and you couldn't sleep at night, Mags and I used to creep into her room. Maggie slept in the armchair because it was enormous and had a footstool and I got into bed with Julie. She didn't mind. It was a double, after all. So we were all in there together and late in the night, the low whirring of the fan and the soft sigh of her breathing, used to lull me to sleep. It was like a lullaby.

Julie told me that she and David were always in the park now because of the tennis. So, one day after school, Mel and I decided to check it out in preparation for the holidays, which were now only a few days away.

The main bit of the park was hopeless for sleuthing, we decided. It was all crew cut lawns - no non-regulation daisies here, thank you - and flower beds that were mostly mud with a few dreary old plants spaced out in rows, standing to attention. They wouldn't have dared do anything else. They were all cut back and watered regularly or heads would roll. Mrs Braden and her kind made sure of that. Even the trees had been given a short back and sides. They looked like broccoli. That part of the park

128

was covered by the busybody patrol. Like the police, they all wore black and kept their poor dogs on a tight leash. Each one of them had a fearsome stare they had been perfecting for centuries. No scope for us there.

But, at the bottom of the slope was a place they never went to and it was fabulous. A stream divided the park in two and the grown ups never crossed it. They couldn't because there wasn't a bridge. We did though because we didn't mind the stepping stones - they were a bit wobbly and covered in moss, so you had to get your legs wet because you were bound to fall in. But that was okay because the stream wasn't very deep. And beyond the stream was the part no-one bothered about. The lawn mowers and the army of gardeners never made it over there. It had run wild. The grass was long and full of wild flowers and the trees were tall and shady. Willows trailed their branches in the stream like the picture in my book of "The Tales of King Arthur". Beyond the trees were open fields. You could walk for hours without seeing anyone or them seeing you. It was perfect. And all it took was a pair of muddy shoes and wet socks.

A quick run down the slope - across the stones and we were there. Our new secret place, hidden from everyone.

Mel and I loved it. We hadn't been there for ages because of the mission. But now the mission was on hold, we were cranking ourselves up for the hols and a place we could explore and make our own. And we could restart the mission because Julie and David were often there too. We could see them sometimes in the distance. But we didn't bother them. Not for the time being. And we reasoned that, although Mum had forbidden us to go to the park, she wouldn't have done if she'd known about Tim and Rusty. Because dogs are man's best friend and will defend you to the death. Everyone knows that. And Tim was a grown up. He was even older than Julie and David. So we were all right there.

Tim and Rusty were in the park nearly every day now. They used to wait for us at the gate by the entrance and we would walk and run together through the trees and across the stream. Tim didn't mind getting wet and Rusty loved it. He didn't bother about the stepping stones. He just plunged right in and splashed across. When he got to the other side he shook himself dry. He soaked us but we didn't mind, he was so lovely. And Tim said it was good for him to run and play ball with us because Red Setters need a lot of exercise. To keep them healthy.

When we got puffed from all the running we would sit together under the trees and Tim would hand out the fruit gums. He brought them for us every day. They got a bit sticky in the heat, but it was a very nice gesture. And although we thought he was a bit funny at first, because he spoke all in a rush and sat a bit too close, he was becoming a real friend. He wasn't good looking at all in his old Airtex shirt and baggy flannels, but he was terrific fun for a grown up. He laughed and yelled just like we did and he was never too busy to be with us. The holidays were going to be bliss, we decided.

* * * * * *

But first there was Sports Day which was going to be ghastly in this heat and a dead loss for a Palmer because we never won any prizes. Maggie was in the tennis team, but only just. She was actually in the reserve, but she carried on like she was Christine Truman and Mum bought her a lovely, white pleated tennis skirt with special knickers to match. Dad was thrilled because he loved sport and our dismal performance in that area was a big disappointment to him. We Juniors were to have a netball match in the morning and some of us were to be ball boys in the Seniors Tennis Match in the afternoon. Mel and I were chosen. By now we were sick of being ball boys, but we were very good at it. Well, we'd had enough practice. I was wondering if we could hire ourselves out at Wimbledon next year. You know, go professional, make some money.

We also considered the bridesmaid business because a lot of weddings happen in the summer. Mel and I had been bridesmaids eleven times between us so we were experts. I had started when I was three. At my cousin Pauline's wedding in Yorkshire. In an apple green frock with a red velvet cape. Honestly. Good job the photos were in black and white. In the middle of the vows I sang "The Grand Old Duke of York" at the top of my voice and Julie, who was the chief bridesmaid, had to take me out. I don't think we'll mention that when we take the bookings. I was only three, after all.

Mel and I talked about all the weddings we had been to, from the lovely ones - my cousin Clive was in the Air Force and at his wedding all his friends and brother officers turned up in their uniforms with swords, which was very exciting as long as they didn't kill each other - to the absolute disasters like Mel's cousin Camilla's, where the bride's mother hated the groom so much that as soon as she'd had a few sherries at the reception, she told him exactly what she thought of him. Loudly. In front of all the guests. One of whom was his mother. They can be terrible things, weddings. You have to know the score, so we figured we'd be an asset because we'd see trouble coming. We could lock the bride's mother up in the Ladies if it looked like the sherries were taking over.

We decided we much preferred being secret agents really, but we were going to be desperate for cash in the holidays because there was so much time to spend it, so all schemes had to be considered.

Sports Day morning was hotter than ever. We went to prayers and then changed into our shorts for netball. While I was changing I noticed that Caro was glaring at me and muttering in my direction like a bear with a sore head, but I took no notice because she never liked me and she was a moron anyway. We played netball all morning and then Caro ran into me and I went flying. That was her revenge for no parley with Julie at the play. I was really hurt. My legs and arms were badly grazed and there

131

was a cut on my cheek which wouldn't stop bleeding. I asked Miss Claire to let me go to hospital but she wouldn't call an ambulance. I had to go to Miss Steed to be cleaned and bandaged up and she made me lie down in the sickroom with a glass of water. When I cried she told me to pull myself together, but I didn't want to, really. What I wanted was a jolly good howl.

At break time Deborah came to see if I was all right, which was decent of her, and when I asked where Mel was, she told me the whole story.

Apparently, after I'd been sent off to Miss Steed, Mel went up to Caro. When I was still there, bleeding all over the place, she'd said nothing, just gone very quiet. That was because she was upset.

Anyway, after I'd gone, she marched up to Caro and called her a big fat bullying bitch and said she'd hurt me deliberately because Julie wouldn't talk to her and nobody worth talking to ever would because she was a brainless cow and vicious with it! And then she reached up and grabbed Caro's plait and tugged it for all she was worth. She swung on it like a bell pull. Deborah thought Mel would scalp Caro. Caro bellowed like a baited bull and then she socked Mel. Miss Claire came running up the field and told Mel she'd never seen such a disgraceful display in all her life and she'd see them both later in the Headmistresses' office.

Wasn't that wonderful? Deborah said she was absolutely gob smacked because she'd always thought Mel was a quiet little mouse who wouldn't say boo to anyone. Well, she'd shown them now all right. Deborah was intrigued, you could tell. I think she wanted to recruit Mel to her gang because although she was a bit runty, she'd proved she could be absolutely deadly. She and I been friends since we were two, when our Mums met taking Maddy and Maggie to Kindergarten, and we were in our pushchairs. I leaned across and pinched her arm and she kicked me. We've been best friends ever since. She's like a sister to me, only better because we understood each other. That doesn't

132

always happen with sisters.

I cried a bit more when Deborah went, thinking of Mel. But then I started to worry because if you were sent to the Headmistresses office, that was serious. The more I thought about it, the worse things looked for Mel. You could get expelled for stuff like that. Because she'd started it and she'd sworn as well. They hated swearing in Heathwood School. You could be like Caro and really hurt people and that was okay. Murder was all right, as long as you didn't swear while you were doing it. Ladies aren't supposed to swear. Whichever way you looked at it, Mel was for it. I decided to take action.

I got up and limped down stairs. My knees really hurt because they were grazed so badly that bending them was agony. My head ached and I felt sick, but I wasn't going to let that stop me. Mel needed me now. That was all that mattered. I rang the bell outside Miss Johnsons' office and then I went in and told her everything.

I told her that Mel was only defending me because Caro had really hurt me and put me in the sickbay when I should be in hospital. But Mel had stuck up for me because she was a true and valiant friend, like the Three Musketeers with "All for one and one for all" - except we're only two, so we have to go at it a bit harder. And they always told us how wonderful Athos, Thingy and Dooda were, so why wasn't Mel when she was only doing the same thing? Miss Johnson listened to me and she could see the cuts and bandages and she said the whole thing was an utter disgrace. She said she was trying to turn us into young ladies and scholars, not thugs and hoodlums. But she did say that she hadn't realised how badly I had been hurt, so she would bear that in mind when dealing with Mel.

So I told her I would get down on my knees if only I could bend them and beg for mercy for Mel because she was my best friend and I couldn't bear the thought of Heathwood School for Girls without her. Then I burst into tears. Miss Johnson put her hand on my shoulder and said she would ring my mother to come and take me home.

But I said I didn't want her to punish Mel without me being there because Mel was sensitive and she shattered easy. Miss Johnson smiled then, a funny twisted up sort of smile that looked as if her mouth wasn't used to it. And she said it didn't look like that to her, but that was quite enough and she would deal with as she saw fit. Then she got Miss Steed to take me back to the sickroom to wait for Mum. And as we walked away, I thought I heard her laughing. But it was such a quiet, creaky little laugh I couldn't tell if I'd really heard it or just thought I did.

So that's how I missed the end of term. I waited for Mum and she took me home. Then she rebandaged me because she never trusted anyone else to nurse us and she frowned and said it looked to her as if there was still some bits of gravel in one knee. She tried to take it out with her eyebrow tweezers, but I screamed so much, she had to stop. But she did say we'd have to keep an eye on it because it could get infected. Then she gave me a Coca Cola and tried to give me a hug. But that wasn't a very good idea because there wasn't a bit of me that didn't hurt, so we gave up. Then she parked me on the sofa with a pile of books, but I didn't want to read. I had started to worry again. Mostly about Mel, but a little bit about me too, in case I had gone too far.

Mel called in on her way home. She told me that Miss Johnson had hauled Caro and her into her office together and told them they were both a disgrace to the school and she'd never heard of such a spectacle in her whole life, let alone in her school. Oh, and if either of them ever dared behave like that again, she'd call the police and they'd be sent straight to Borstal. For good. As it was, she could see it was six of one and half a dozen of the other, but I was the injured one so Caro would have to write a letter of apology to me and read it out in front of the whole class on the first day of next term. I couldn't wait for that one.

Then she said Mel had behaved appallingly, but at least she was defending her friend, and if she ever caught either of them in her office again for anything, anything at all, she'd have them out of this school so fast their feet wouldn't touch the ground. Did they understand? They did. Mel would be in detention every week for the first month of the new term. Was that clear? It was. And she would write to their parents. She finished up by saying that never again would she allow one of her pupils to go home in bandages because they'd been attacked by another. And that was final. Then she dismissed them.

So Mel would have to tell her mother before the letter came. She was terrified, she said, but not sorry. She was a real brick. And she asked me if I would speak to her Mum and tell her what had happened and I promised I would. It was the least I could do. Then she went home to try and rack up some brownie points before the axe fell.

When Maggie came home she told me that she'd heard all about it at school. How Mel had gone beserk and Caroline had nearly killed me. She asked Mum to take off the bandages so she could see "the extent of my injuries", but Mum wouldn't.

Then she said I looked just like "unty Katy with bandages up both legs. She could be so mean, Maggie, but when I got up to go to the loo she saw how much it hurt me to walk and she went all quiet. She was waiting for me in the hall when I came out and she asked me if I could manage. I said yes, but it really hurt.

So she said she would go upstairs and fetch my crayons and stuff for me and it was okay to want Ted. She'd bring him as well. Then she told me if I wanted a drink or some biscuits just to ask her. Oh and if I felt hot, she'd come and take my temperature because she needed the practice.

Dad went crazy when he came home and saw me. He said he wasn't paying all this money to have me beaten to a pulp.

He said that Heathwood School for Girls was not supposed to be a correctional facility in the Gorbals. He was really angry. But not with me because he kept stroking my head. Mum said she had complained to Miss Johnson and she had promised Mum she would take "appropriate action". But Dad said he'd take appropriate action if he ever ran into Miss Caroline Harris.

He'd show her what the word bully really meant. And his eyes were angry and his mouth set in a thin, hard line. Dad can be quite scary when he's cross.

I had gone to bed by the time Julie came home, but Mum must have told her because she crept in to see me.

"You asleep, Tink?"

"No."

"Why not?"

"Hurts too much". And she went and came back with a glass of water and an aspirin. And then she brought her fan and set it up in my room so I wouldn't be too hot in the night. She took the sheet off me because even that hurt. Then she gave me a kiss. She was horrified. You could tell. No-one had ever tried to kill one of her sisters before.

* * * * * *

The next morning Mum had to take me to the doctor. My knee had swollen up and was red and sore. Watery stuff was coming out. I was leaking. This was an emergency. They had to get me to Dr Rees Jones right away.

Fortunately he only lived four doors down the road from us and his surgery was in his house, in a sort of annexe. When we got there he saw me straight away.

He looked at my knee and said: "Sorry, old girl. I'm going to have to get that gravel out". He wasn't half as sorry as I was.

The nurse came in with a bowl of water and he sort of washed it, which was bad enough but then he started picking bits of gravel out with a big version of Mum's eyebrow tweezers. It was horrific. It hurt so much I thought I would wet my pants. And when I looked at Mum she had gone all white and looked as if she wasn't far off wetting hers, either. My teeth were busy grinding, but nothing stopped it hurting. Dr Rees Jones was very nice. He kept saying sorry. In the end it was over and my head ached and I wondered if I had any teeth left. I might have ground them down to the stumps. Then he painted the whole knee with iodine, which made it go bright yellow and felt as it he was burning it right off. I was getting depressed now. It was hopeless. You couldn't be a movie star with only one leg. You probably couldn't be a secret agent, either. I decided to grasp the nettle. I knew what was what. I watched "Emergency Ward Ten."

"Will I lose the leg, doctor?" I managed to spit the words out through my gritted teeth and he laughed at me! That man had no heart. Well, he was Deborah's father. They probably pulled the wings off flies and tortured baby birds together at the weekend. Mum looked at me as if I'd gone mad, but I didn't care. It was my leg. I had to know if I was going to end up like "Chester" in "Matt Dillon" for the rest of my life.

"No, Sally, your leg will be fine. But it will hurt for a bit. I'll put a dressing on and then give you a little jab."

"Why?"

It was almost a scream. An injection as well! What had I done to deserve this? I must have been Jack The Ripper last time around. Mum nodded. It was all right for her.

" Lockjaw" she whispered to me as he prepared the needle. I'd had enough.

"There's nothing wrong with my jaw. Only my knee." I meant to sound firm, but it came out like a kind of bleat.

"Yes, Sally, but the ground where you fell was dirty and we don't want you catching anything nasty."

"I didn't fall. I was pushed". I must have scowled when I thought of Caro because he softened up, "I know, old thing. Not your day." He could say that again. Mum smiled her "Be brave." smile at me and Dr Rees Jones began his bandaging. He did it very well. All neat and tight with no loose bits, folded round in

137

a kind of pattern. Mags could pick up a few tips from him. She had practised her bandaging on me once and it was either so tight I went blue or so saggy it fell off.

While Dr Rees Jones was bandaging, I looked at him. He was very like Deborah. Which was odd because he was old and a man and she was young and a girl. But they had the same shape mouth and nose and the same colour eyes, a sort of bluey grey. But he had hair in his ears and she didn't.

His hands were very rough. That was because of all the washing. Doctors have to be terribly clean. Mags had told me that. Or they could kill off half their patients, she said, maybe more. She washed her hands all the time. Practising, she said, for the future. Then came the jab. All I can say about that is I only screamed a bit.

When Dr Rees Jones had finished, he opened the door and called up into the house for Deborah. She came and sat with me in the waiting room while Mum talked to her dad. I told her all about my knee, how it had swollen up and leaked and how her Dad had to pick the bits out from an open wound and give me an injection for my jaw as well. Then Deborah looked cross. She liked her subjects to be alive and Caro was wiping them out. Then she said that Mel was right! Caro was completely brainless and nasty with it, and she'd much rather have a friend who would stick up for you against all the odds than a moron like Caro. Really, she said that. Honestly. In the waiting room. You could tell she thought it was time to jump ship because she asked me then if she could come over and play with Mel and me sometime during the holidays!!! And I ummed and ah'ed and said well, we were a bit busy at the moment with our secret mission (which was a lie), and I had to spare some time for the man she had seen at the play. The one in the grey suit. The one who had kissed me and taken the afternoon off She looked a bit puzzled then.

"I thought he was your sister's boyfriend."

"Yes, he is. We ... er... sort of share him." That foxed her. Then I said that on the other hand, the summer holidays

138

were very long and we were only going away for two weeks to Paignton at the end of August, so I was sure we could fit her in somewhere. If we juggled a bit. And do you know what she said, "Thanks Sall."!!!!! Thank you from Deborah, who never thanked anyone, Deborah, who would take your last Smartie if you were starving!!

So we smiled at each other and then Mum came out of the Doctors office and we limped home. Well, I did anyway. Mum held my hand, which was a bit embarrassing. In case Deborah was watching.

So I was out of action. And for a few days, I was parked on the sofa for most of the time because moving around really hurt. And while I was parked, stuck on the sofa at the very start of the holidays, I thought about Caro.

I hated her. I wished her the most horrible death at the hands of a fiend without mercy. A fiend driven mad by suffering. Me. I read "Tales of King Arthur" and pretended I was Morgan Le Fay. I cursed Caro good and proper. I spent hours doing it. And then I got fed up with it because it is really very boring to go on cursing and cursing. It takes a lot of energy. And then Mel came round to visit and she brought me a bag of all my favourite sweets. Because she knows better than anyone what I like best. Sherbert fountains and bubble gum and lots of little pink seahorse chews. So that was all right.

We talked about our plans for the summer. And how if we could only get into Mums' car, we could play "Route 66" and travel across America without moving my knee at all. Because for the time being, the park was out for me. So that seemed a good idea and much better than silly old Morgan Le Fay and her endless cursing.

It didn't take us long to suss it out. Mum didn't lock her car in the daytime when it was in the drive. So after she came back from her shopping, which she did early now because of the heat, the car was more or less ours as long as she didn't spot us. Because then she'd go crazy. But she was usually in the kitchen and the back of the house and even Mum couldn't see through brick walls. She did all her stuff, cleaning, cooking, washing, tidying everything up, thinking we were in the living room playing Monopoly with the door closed. But we weren't. We were in her car. We'd lay out the board and out we'd go through the French windows which were always open now because of the weather. It was our secret.

* * * * * *

We played "Route 66" in the car for hours roaming across America with Tod Stiles and Buz Murdock. We liked the blonde freckled one best. Buz. He looked a bit like Tim - only more handsome and much better dressed.

We always had a good old session in the afternoon, before tea. Because after that was a bit dodgy. We had to scarper before Dad got home. He had strictly forbidden us to play in the car. But we decided to apply his ban only to his car. So we were obeying him really. Sort of.

But I didn't want to test him out because I had the feeling that if he found us in Mum's car, walking wouldn't be the only difficulty. Sitting down might become a challenge. And pocket money would probably be withheld until I was as old as Aunty Katy. But only if he found out. So we made sure he didn't.

A police car began to drive round the Circle, patrolling the area. That was new. Perhaps Lockheart was back on the scene. And that worried us because playing in the car was probably against the law and we didn't want to get arrested. So we made sure "Route 66" was over before they appeared.

Late one afternoon, Mel and I and Tod Stiles and Buz Murdock were driving across America. It was absolutely boiling. We were in the Arizona desert, complete with those big versions of the prickly plants Mum has in a china bowl in the sitting room. And rattlesnakes and no water. We were in an awful bind, but we were going on regardless.

140

Just as we were approaching The Grand Canyon and a wise old Indian was about to show us the only water source in a thousand miles, David walked past on his way to meet Julie. I waved, but I went on with the game because we were just getting to the best bit and we hadn't got much time. He came up to the car.

"Where are you off to, Sall?"

"We're in the Grand Canyon on our way to New Orleans." He looked a bit blank. No imagination, that boy. Then he opened the back door and got in.

"Got room for me and Julie?" Mel turned round and smiled at him. "You bet." She'd liked David ever since he let her win at pogo.

"Good. I'll help out with the driving. It's very big, America. Wake me up when we get to Santa Fe." He slouched down and pretended to go to sleep. So, he wasn't that gormless, after all. We drove on through the desert. It wasn't hard to imagine. It was like an oven in that car. Even with all the windows open. Then Julie walked by, waved at us and did a sort of double take when she saw David in the back seat.

"Have you gone stark staring mad?"

"Yup. Do you want to meet Elvis? How d'you feel about a honeymoon in Memphis?" She stared at him for a minute and then started to laugh. He opened the car door.

"Come on in." He patted the seat beside him.

"You're bonkers. Mum'll see us. Get out of the bloody car."

David slid across the back seat towards her. Then he leaned over on his way out and put his hand on my shoulder.

"Heard about your run in with the Human Hulk, Sall. We're planning a treat. But for now, I used to know this crazy kid who hid behind plants and liked these." And he dropped the biggest bag of pear drops you've ever seen into my lap. Then he went off to the park with Julie. He really was the most wonderful man. Julie was right. He was a dreamboat. Even if he did have funny hair.

141

* * * * * *

Two days after that the treat came. It was a Saturday. Julie got off work early and David didn't work at all on Saturdays. They were taking me to the cinema. The big one in Harrow. To see "101 Dalmatians", which I had longed to see for ages. It was going to be just perfect.

Julie dressed us both up. She wore her white floaty dress with no shoulders and the swimsuit top that she wore when she went to get David back after the Big Gesture. The skirt was made up of lots of very thin layers of stuff that was nearly see through. That was what made it floaty. It was called chiffon, Julie said. I wished I had one. But I didn't.

I didn't have anything except my pink party dress that was a bit too small and showed all the bandages. So Julie said it wouldn't do and she went and rummaged in Maggie's wardrobe and bullied her into lending me her best blue skirt with the little red boats on. It was really nice, a full, swishy skirt with a matching white shirt with red and blue trimmings. The skirt was long enough to hide the bandages, but we had to do it up with a safety pin because it was too big. The shirt was okay because Maggie had no more bosoms than I did and a bit baggy doesn't matter. Julie did my hair and slicked some pale pink lipstick across my lips, but not so much that Mum would get the wind up. So I felt really very nice and smart for my outing.

We took the bus into Harrow, which was a bit difficult for me. I had to stand up all the way because it was less painful. But I also had to make sure no-one bashed into me with their shopping bags because that would have been agony.

Outside the Odeon Cinema David was waiting for us. He had made a special effort too. In spite of the heat, he wore a black jacket with a lovely white shirt that had metal tips on the

142

collar and a thin tie that was more like a ribbon and tied in a bow. He looked just like Wyatt Earp on the telly. He still had his pointy old shoes on, which were a bit weird, but he could hardly have worn lace-ups with that getup. Cowboy boots and silver spurs would have been more like it. Still, you can't have everything. Silver spurs might have been a bit of a hazard on the bus.

It really was going to be the most marvellous treat. We went into the cinema. Julie queued up and bought the tickets while David and I went to buy the ice creams. And he bought me a Kia Ora orange drink too! Then we went in. Julie had bought really good seats. Front row of the balcony. They were very expensive, but she said she had bought them so I wouldn't have to sit with my knee all cramped up. There would be tons of room for me to stretch my leg out and be comfortable. She could be very thoughtful when she wanted to be, Julie. We ate the ice creams right away so they wouldn't melt while the adverts were on and then the film began. I couldn't wait to see it. It was going to be absolutely super.

It was a cartoon film by Walt Disney, but I already knew the story because I had read the book.

I loved the film. Well, I had loved the book. I thought it was the most wonderful story - how Pongo and Missis searched everywhere for their stolen puppies and all the dogs of England helped to rescue them through the Twilight Barking. I couldn't stop talking about it when we came out of the cinema and on the bus on the way home. David and Julie liked it too. They pretended to be all grown up and said it was a bit babyish for them, but I saw Julie wipe away a tear when she thought the puppies were lost and David looked horrified when Cruella de Vil said she wanted the puppies for fur coats.

But the treat wasn't over. We got the bus back and David helped me to get down and then he walked straight into the brand new Chinese restaurant that had just opened in the Kenton Road. There were lots of people there. It was very crowded. We took the only empty table left. It was a fabulous place. It

143

was called "The Lotus House" and it was so new that even Mum and Dad hadn't been there yet.

It was terribly smart. Inside was quite dark with these funny lanterns that hung low over the table so you could see what you got. I had never been anywhere like it in my life. There were these panel things on the wall - Julie said they were made of silk! - with Chinese scenes painted on them. Mostly funny looking boats and willow trees. And the rest of the walls were covered in a sort of wooden trellis thing like you grow plants up, only this was painted a bricky sort of red. When you sat down they brought you tea, which was a bit of a disappointment because I had wanted Coke, but the tea came in a sweet teapot with a bamboo handle and the little blue and white cups had no handles at all! The china was so thin you could almost see through it. It was like a very beautiful doll's tea set. Then they brought us these wonderful white crisp things, which were called prawn crackers and they were gorgeous! I ate most of them.

David let Julie order the meal because we hadn't been to a Chinese restaurant before and she had, so she knew the ropes. And we had something called Chow Mein which was a sort of delicious chicken and noodle thing, and a wonderful fried pork in a kind of pineapple jam and funny rice with egg and peas in it and these lovely crunchy things called bamboo shoots. It was superb.

We laughed a lot because Julie and David were always joking and it was so wonderful and new. We had a lot of fun. I had never had a meal in a restaurant that was fun before. It all tended to get a bit solemn with Mum and Dad because you really had to be on best behaviour with manners and napkins and elbows to the fore.

There was none of that here. David had his elbows on the table and I dropped my napkin. No-one cared. We laughed and joked so much that I got hiccups and everyone looked at us and then we had to pipe down and remember our manners. We weren't Mum trained for nothing.

144

The whole thing was absolutely wonderful. Julie ate her meal with two sticks. They were called chopsticks and that's what Chinese people eat with. Honestly. Julie knew how to use them. She made us try too, but she nearly cried with laughter at David, who was even worse than I was. He just could not get any of his food to stay on the sticks for long enough for him to eat it. He tried and tried and then he said he surrendered and now he knew what Chinese Torture really was. It was trying to pick up grains of rice with a stick and could he have a fork and spoon, please. So we both did, him and me, but Julie went on with the sticks because she could actually eat with them.

For pudding we had ice cream and a wonderful white fruit that looked like pickled onions and tasted like bath salts. They were called lychees and they were heaven.

David looked at Julie eating her ice cream and mouthed "I love you" at her and she said "I love you too" out loud. The lady at the next table stared at us, but we didn't care. It's rude to stare, anyway. Then Julie and David held hands across the table and she was wearing his ring! So I said "Are you engaged now?" and he said, "Sort of", and she said "Yes". So I congratulated them and drank their health in Chinese tea because I had some left. It's not actually very nice, Chinese tea. It tastes a bit like wet straw, but I didn't say anything because the meal was fabulous and they were being so nice. Then David said he was having dinner with his two favourite girls and what could be better? And that made me very happy because it meant that he did love me a little bit, too.

When the meal was over we walked home slowly and talked about the film. I said I had adored it, but I was a bit disappointed that my favourite bit in the book had been left out. David said he supposed they couldn't put everything from the book into the film or it would run for about three weeks! He could be very funny. He always saw things in a different way from other people. Then Julie asked me what my favourite bit was and I told her it was the chapter called "Buttered Toast" when Pongo and Missis shelter in a ghostly old house and are

145

helped by a very old man and his Spaniel. They sleep in a four poster bed and the old man thinks they are the ghosts of the Dalmatians of the past because his house is full of ghosts.

So that started us off talking about ghosts and haunted houses and David started to tease us and clown about, making spooky sounds to frighten us. I didn't like it. The light was peculiar. It didn't get properly dark now and nothing looked the right size. The pale shapes of the roses in the front gardens seemed to loom out of the shadows and the street lamps had a horrid orange glow. I thought I heard footsteps that weren't ours and suddenly, I felt afraid. I felt as if someone else was there, someone we couldn't see, someone watching us. I stopped to listen and David jumped out from behind a tree and I screamed.

Julie got very cross with him. I think it was because she'd got spooked too, but she told him to cut it out and couldn't he see he was really scaring me?

So David laughed and said, "Julie, I couldn't scare Sally. She's more likely to scare me!" And I laughed too because it was a kind of a compliment and I could tell he only meant it to stop me feeling silly. We walked on and I began to calm down.

By the time we got to the gate, I didn't feel silly at or scared anymore. I had had the most wonderful evening of my life, my knee had even forgotten to hurt and I told them that and we all had a hug together and I said thank you with all my heart. Because it had been the best treat anyone ever had. The very best ever. They looked very pleased when I said that. Then I went in and left them alone to say goodnight.

* * * * * *

When Maggie got home the next morning I told her all about it. Everything. She had spent the night with her friend Sharon, who lived in Barn Hill. She often spent the night there or Sharon came to us because Maggie wasn't lucky like me, her best friend didn't live "on her doorstep" as Dad called it, like Mel did. Sharon lived a bus ride away.

When I told her about the restaurant, she went very quiet. She got that serious look that meant she wasn't happy. I thought at first it was because she was jealous or fed up about lending me her skirt, but that wasn't really fair because she had been to stay with Sharon and Julie had bought her that beautiful dress for the dance. She just said less and less. Then she shut up completely. I couldn't work out what was bugging her. She wasn't usually jealous and she didn't mind lending things. In the end I couldn't stand the silence. I always cracked first. I asked her what was the matter. She sighed.

"They're not even trying to keep it a secret anymore, are they?"

That shook me. "No. Not really."

There was no point in lying to Mags. She could always tell. She was like Dad, they had a sort of built in radar. They could spot a lie blipping away on the horizon. We were sitting at the kitchen table, having a Ribena. Mum was upstairs, hoovering. Mags rested her head on one hand and stared out of the window.

"Are you worried that Mum and Dad will find out?"

She shook her head. "Oh no, they'll find out all right. Sooner rather than later, I imagine. Some old biddy in the restaurant will be dying to tell Mum." I hadn't thought of that. I'd been too busy having a good time. Then she looked me straight in the eye and went on. "That's not what matters ".

I could never follow Maggie' train of thought. She went twice as far and twice as fast as anyone else in the human race.

"What do you mean? What matters?"

"Jeannie. How long do you think it will be before someone tells Jeannie?"

CHAPTER 12

It was getting very boring, the way Margaret Palmer was always right. I didn't understand what was going on at all.

The next morning, I did try to warn Julie, but I didn't get very far. She wouldn't let me. I went into her bedroom when she was dressing. I hung around looking out of the window to see if I could see David and then I said. " Don't you think you ought to hide a bit more? Just to keep the secret." Because she still hadn't told Mum. David appeared at the very end of the road. A tiny speck that was getting bigger.

Julie stopped rummaging through her wardrobe and turned around. She only had her knickers on. They were very nice. White, lacy things. She shook her head.

"No, Sall. We're not hiding any more." And then she smiled a "go away, child, you can't possibly understand " sort of smile and that was all she would say.

So it was very confusing because just at the moment they had gone public and stopped hiding, for me they had suddenly gone private, because she wouldn't talk about it anymore. She flatly refused to.

I had no idea what was going on in their minds. Julie was behaving as if Jeannie didn't exist. I suppose she just put it out of her mind and carried on. Because thinking about it and not carrying on had hurt too much. So she didn't. I had no idea what David thought either. Except he was in love with Julie and he wasn't going to give her up. That was obvious. But he hadn't given Jeannie up either. It was a terrific muddle.

Now the mission was on ice, there wasn't much I could do to protect them. Perhaps we were all biding our time. But we couldn't bide it forever. Because soon a baby would be born.

149

* * * * * *

After we'd been on holiday for about a week, I began to feel better. My knee was much less sore and had begun to itch. Mags said that was "a good sign." The bruises were fading nicely, too. They were pale green and yellow now instead of black and blue.

The bandages came off and were replaced by a white sort of dressing thing that was stuck on with plasters. Much better. More stream-lined. The holidays had only just begun and Caro had only really robbed me of a week. I decided to take matters in hand. Looking at myself in the big mirror in the bathroom, I realised that I had let things go to pot in the glamour department. Well, it had been a bit difficult trying to look sexy after Caro'd turned me into something from "The Return of the Mummy", but that was over now and it was time to try again.

I decided to have another bash at glamour. It wasn't easy. I roped Mel in. She looked like she could do with a bit of glamour too. But we were operating under serious restrictions. We weren't allowed make up because Mum would go bananas. We couldn't wear sexy clothes because we hadn't got bosoms. Yet. And Mum wouldn't let us wear shoes with even tiny heels (like Janet Elkins had) because she said they looked "common", so we didn't have those either. But we had to make a start somewhere.

After lunch one day, when it was really too hot to play in the garden, and Maggie was out at Sharon's and Mum was having a lie down on the sofa because this heat was "so exhausting", we went into Julie's room and shut the door. Because if we couldn't pick up a few glamour tips in there, we were a lost cause. We roamed round opening drawers and

150

having a rummage, when I had my brain wave. We would wash each other's hair and set it on Julie's big squashy rollers that she kept in the top drawer of her dressing table. It would dry in no time in this heat.

So we did that and we had a really good foam fight with the shampoo and then we put Julie's Creme Rinse on to make our hair shine, like the lady on the label. Except it didn't. My hair went like Maggie's when she hasn't washed it, so perhaps we didn't rinse it out properly. Anyway, we couldn't waste all day on that so we curled it up, which wasn't easy. We kept most of the curlers in place with about fifty metal pins, then we went and sat on the balcony to wait for it to dry. Hoping that no-one with a magnet would walk by.

But waiting is very boring, so we came back in and had another rummage. To see if we could scrounge any make-up that Mum's eagle eye couldn't spot and while we were doing it, I had my inspiration.

"Got it!" I had opened the wrong drawer by mistake, looking for lipstick, and the answer was lying there. Right in front of my eyes.

"Got what?" Mel was trying Julie's earrings on. She had a white daisy one on one ear and a glittery drop thing on the other. She looked really daft.

"The common factor, idiot."

Mel looked a bit worried. She thought I was talking about sums. She wasn't very good at those. I decided to put her out of her misery.

"The one thing all ladies have and we don't."

"Bosoms?"

"Nope. Try again."

She looked blank. I sighed. It was pitiful. I tried another tack. "What keeps us firmly in the kiddie brigade?"

"I dunno." She pulled one earing off and winced as it pinched her ear.

"SOCKS, you great dope, white regulation ankle SOCKS! " I was hopping about on one foot, ripping mine off.

"And what do lovely sexy ladies have instead?"

"STOCKINGS!" I pointed to the open drawer. And there lying neatly stacked were two brand new, still in the packet, pairs of Kayser Bonder stockings, size eight and a half. They were called "American Tan" and they were going to make us gorgeous..

Mel looked doubtful. "We can't take those, Sally. They haven't even been opened yet. In any case, we haven't got any suspenders."

See what I mean? She was hopeless. If the Pilgrim Fathers had been like her, they'd never have got out of Plymouth.

I tried to remember something Dad was always telling us, but I couldn't because I never listen. Something about faint heart never winning a fair lady. They talk awful bilge, grownups.

"So? What are safety pins for?"

I took both packets out and laid them on the bed. There was a real glamour puss on the cover. With long, tanned, silky legs. Me. If only I had the nerve. I decided I did - because no-one ever made it to Hollywood by being scared of their big sister.

I opened the first packet and took out the stockings. "Don't you want to look wonderful? Just for a little while? We can wear them for a bit and then put them back. She'll never know." But I was what Mum called "preaching to the converted". I had seen the look on Mel's face when I took out the first stocking. I 'd got her. She was hooked.

"All right, then. There are some safety pins in here," and she fished around in the chocolate box, Terrys Gold, that Julie kept her jewellery in and brought out two safety pins.

"I think we'll need more." I was already smoothing a stocking up one leg. They felt lovely. Soft, silky, sheer. Heaven. We did need more pins because the stockings were far too long. We fixed them to our knickers with the safety pins, but we needed two a leg to make sure they stayed up. Because they tended to sag and go wrinkly round the knees with just one. They looked FABULOUS. So did we. This was more like it.

We took our hair out of the rollers. Some of the curls fell out straight away, but not all of them and it smelled super, like orange blossom. So we drowned it all in Julie's hair spray because that's what grownups always do when their hair's a bit skewiff.

As we were creeping downstairs, and not even a whisper so as not to wake Mum, I started a day dream. Perhaps David would see us as we walked by. (Daft because his office was miles away, but day dreams always are a bit silly, aren't they?). He would see me and be struck dumb by my beauty and my wonderful legs in the "American Tan". Perhaps he would keep me in mind for the future. When Julie was off being an international skating star again.

Then I thought about me being a star. In Hollywood. Where there would be palm trees and cars with no roof and I would go to places like the Chinese restaurant in Kenton all the time. And eat weird things in the dark and drink tea from cups with no handles. Maybe I'd even learn to eat with those stick things. It was going to be wonderful. All of it.

By now we had reached the back door. As we walked out Mel said, "Where are we going?" and I had to think quickly because I hadn't actually got that far. We decided that we would go to the fish and chip shop for threepence worth of chips to share, because that was all we could afford and then on for a turn around the park. So everyone could see us and notice how grown up and glamorous we had become. But we'd have to stick to the main part of the park because the stepping stones would be the end of the "American Tan".

As we were walking, I looked down again. My legs looked super, sort of longer and more shapely. 'Course, we only had our school sandals on, and you don't normally wear those with stockings, but nobody ever looks at feet anyway. We walked on to the fish and chip shop. I wished I had brought Maggie's little white bag too - the one Julie brought her from

Paris - to complete the ensemble, but you can't think of everything.

We went into the fish and chip shop and stood around, but no-one seemed to notice our legs. There was hardly any one in there. It was too hot. So we stood it for a while to give the man behind the counter time to admire us, and we smiled encouragingly at him and kept looking down at our legs, but he didn't twig. He just asked if we wanted anything or were we going to stand there all day, so we ordered our chips. He was horrible, anyway. Short, fat, going bald. And he had batter on his apron. No point in impressing him.

The only other person in there was Mr Nicholls, who came every day for the pensioner's special offer. He always had his lunch in the afternoon. He was very old and had lived alone since his sister died. He wore spats and a panama hat. That told you everything really. He nodded at us, but he had a mouthful of cod, so there wasn't much conversation to be had out of him. In any case, his admiring days were long gone. So we took our chips and went outside.

The chips were very good. We went into the park, but by the time we got there disaster had struck. I looked down to admire my "American Tan" and saw a big hole in one leg. A ladder was running all the way down from above my knee to my ankle. I looked across to check Mel. Her "American Tan" seemed to be all right. Then I looked at mine and panicked.

"Oh God! What are we going to do? Julie will kill us!"

"She'll kill you. Mine are okay." I hated Mel sometimes.

"Well, you're in it too. I'm not wearing two pairs of stockings, am I?" She turned her back on me and started hop-scotching down the path. Then I spotted it. A tiny ladder was running all the way down the back of her right leg.

"Look at the back of your leg, clever clogs."

She twisted round and saw it. Now she looked like I felt.

"Perhaps we could buy her some more."

"What with? We'd have to rob a bank first."

The prospect did not look good. Then Mr Nicholls

154

strolled by. He often went for a walk after his lunch. He called it his "Constitutional". He raised his hat and waved at us. He always perked up a bit after his cod and chips. I was too depressed even to wave back. Then Mrs Braden appeared on the horizon with Secundo. That was terrible because she was a witness. As she walked past we said "Hello, Mrs Braden" and she stared at our legs and glared at us, shaking her head and tutting. She really was a frightful old bat. Even in this weather, she still wore her old black hat and coat. The only concession was the fox. He'd been left at home. Either that or Secundo had got him. She walked away briskly. On her way back to tell Mel's Mum she'd seen us in the park in stockings! We were for it. Our only hope was that she might drop dead of heat stroke on the way home.

We sat there in silence, wearing very expensive ladders. Then to our delight Tim and Rusty appeared. Rusty bounded straight over to us, barking and jumping up, but Tim took one look at us and seemed absolutely gob-smacked. He couldn't stop staring at our legs. Perhaps we did look a bit dishy after all.

He walked up to us and just stood there, then finally he said, "Hello, you two. Long time no see. Where've you been?"

"Someone tried to kill her." said Mel.

"I was a medical emergency," I announced. Anything to get my mind off the medical emergency Julie was going to turn me into when I got home.

"Golly. What happened?" So I told him all about Caro and Dr Rees Jones, but he wasn't listening. He was still staring at our legs. This was getting to be too much of a good thing. A bit of a gawp is okay, nice even, but staring like that is just rude. I tried to get him to talk, but nothing doing. In the end I got cross.

"Earth to Tim? Do you read me? Hallo Alien Craft, anybody there?" Mel gasped. I was being terribly rude. Especially to a grown up. But I was worried sick and he was the limit.

"Sorry, Sally. I ..." and he frowned and then he pulled

155

himself together and came back and sat down on the bench beside us.

"That Caro bitch needs teaching a good lesson, if you ask me." That was more like it.

"My sentiments exactly, my dear Watson."

I don't think he knew who Watson was but he at least he seemed to have found his marbles.He looked down at my legs for a long time and then up into my face and said, "You need a bit of a rescue, sweetie."

And his voice had gone soft and husky, the way men's do when they like you, and I began to feel sorry for snapping at him. Perhaps he was trying to be a true friend after all. He was a bit peculiar, but perhaps it was just his way.

"What I need is a one way ticket to Timbuktoo." He looked puzzled. "Julie is going to go kill me when she finds out."

"Why?"

"Cos they're hers."

"Oh. Who's Julie?"

"My sister. Her boyfriend's in the Mafia." I didn't really think David would do anything, but Julie was another story. Tim went quiet and sort of thoughtful and then he pulled out the fruit gums and we all had one.

"Look, you can trust me, okay? I'll sort it out for you. Don't worry."

Then he stood up. "I'll buy you some more."

"But they're terribly expensive!" Shut up, Mel!

"Never mind. I'll buy some for this Julie and some for you. Then you can wear yours just for me. It'll be our little secret."

"But what shall we do about these?" Mel was in wailing mode. She was getting on my nerves.

"Nothing. They're finished. Take 'em off."

"We can't do that. You can't undress in the park."

"Hide behind those trees. Come on, no-one will see you."

For someone who was not quite the full 16 ounces, Tim suddenly seemed to be very much on the ball. Cool as you like he strolled over the grass towards the trees. He kept guard while we hid behind a tree and pulled our skirts up. Then we unpinned the stockings from our knickers. I was having trouble with mine because the pin had got tangled up in the hole and Tim offered to help.

He put his hand on the top of my leg and yanked the pin away, and the edge of my knickers tore.

Then he gripped my hand really hard and said, "You can't tell anyone about this. Not even your Mother. Or I can't help you. Understand?" I nodded. "Good. I'll see you tomorrow."

Then he rolled the stockings up into a ball and put them in his pocket and walked away.

"Do you think Tim's okay?" Mel was pulling her skirt down.

"Course he is."

"Then why can't you tell your mother?"

I turned on her then because I didn't know either.

"You're such a baby, Mel. You don't know anything, do you? You can't tell your mother about men. No-one ever does."

She went bright red and looked a bit teary. The whole thing had been too much for her. It had been too much for me too, but I couldn't say anything because it was my idea. So we went home and played very quietly. And I let her be Captain Cook and have the only biscuit left with pink icing on because I had been so rotten. After all, it wasn't her fault. It was mine.

* * * * * *

Trouble was never very long in coming in our house. The next morning I was sitting up in bed reading my comic. It always came on a Wednesday. I didn't want to get up just yet. I

157

had a funny sort of tummy ache that kept moving about into my back. It was very peculiar. I was just settling into the "Bunty" when the door opened. Julie stood in the doorway. She was furious. It looked as if Tim's rescue was going to be too late.

"All right, where are they?"

I decided to try and fend her off.

"Where's what?"

You know. My stockings. My Kayser Bonder. My American Tan."

Suddenly, I felt very hot. She went on, "Look, Sally, I know it's you."

"How?" She wasn't Maggie. How did she know?

"Because they won't fit Mum and Maggie doesn't steal. And she wouldn't wear two pairs of stockings even if she did. You steal all the time and you and Mel are joined at the hip." Dad must have made her read Sherlock too.

"So where are they?" She started to opening all the drawers in my dresser. She wouldn't find anything in there. I started to say I was sorry.

"What have you done with them?" I had to tell her.

She was livid. "You really are the bloody end! Do you have any idea how much they cost?" The earth. You could tell from her face. She was so cross she was hopping about with rage, like Rumpelstiltskin.

"I take you to the flicks, AND for a Chinese! I spend a bloody fortune on you because you've grazed your knee and this is what I get! You ungrateful thieving little brat! You follow me round like a bloody shadow and I even come to your stupid play! I do everything I can for you. Well, no more, sister!" She stormed back towards the door.

"And if I ever catch you in my room again, you'll wish you'd never been born. Like the rest of us do."

And she slammed the door on her way out. Just like Cruella de Vil.

She didn't even let me tell her about Tim and the rescue. She could be very spiteful, Julie. The thought that everyone in

158

the family wished I'd never been born really hurt my feelings. So I sat for a bit and then went into Mum. She was already dressed and sitting at her dressing table, powdering her nose.

"Mum, do you wish I'd never been born?"

She must have heard the shouting and the door slam, but she was doing what she did with all our fights. Unless we hit each other, she just ignored it. She turned around with the powder puff still in her hand. "What a silly idea! What's got into you, Sally? What have you done now?"

See, Julie was right. Even Mum didn't deny it. I went into the bathroom for a pee, but Maggie was already in there brushing her teeth.

"Do you wish I'd never been born?"

"All the time. Why?" She spat into the basin. I sat down to have my pee.

"I took Julie's stockings. Two pairs - for Mel and me. I thought we'd just borrow them and bring them back and she'd never know, but they went all laddery and then they got holes in them, so we had to throw them away. And now she says you all wish I'd never been born." And I started to bawl.

"Sally, you are such a twit." She was laughing at me again, with toothpaste all round her mouth. I cried harder. And my stomach hurt.

"You always do these really stupid things and you always get found out. How could you imagine she wouldn't notice? Two pairs!"

She wiped her mouth on the towel. I wiped my bottom. Then I screamed. There was blood all over the paper. "Maggie, I'm bleeding to death!" She came over with a sort of embarrassed smile on her face.

"No, you're not. You've just started, that's all." She opened the cupboard door and rummaged about inside. She didn't seem very concerned.

"Started what?" I was dying. They'd be sorry now. "Go and get Mum! Call an ambulance!"

She sighed and handed me a box of Dr White's.

"What's that for?"

"You. You'll need them from now on." And she went to get Mum.

The rest of the day was very peculiar. Mum bundled me up with this cotton wool nappy thing and I bled on it. All day long. She flatly refused to get an ambulance, but gave me this talk instead about how it was quite normal and natural, and only to be expected even though I was a little young, but everyone varied a bit. Oh, and I would do this once a month until I was an old woman. Even after I had babies. Then she tried to tell me about the facts of life, but I told her not to bother because Deborah Rees Jones already had. She looked a bit cross about that, but not for long because then she said that I was really starting to grow up now. And for a moment she looked sad, but then she cheered up and said I was still her baby and always would be and how about some cinnamon toast? She said her mother used to make it for her because cinnamon was good for cramps. So I got the toast, but I also had this. They were very hot, these pad things, and when you bled on them they smelled a bit, so you had to change them a lot. And it wasn't like measles, that you only got once, this was for life. It was dreadful. I couldn't wait to ring Mel. Because I'd got mine first.

She was a bit miffed. Normally, she likes being first. But I'd pipped her to the post with this one. She came over right away and spent the day with me. We couldn't go to the park because I was suffering and in any case, poor old Tim was too late. Cruella de Jules had already struck. So we played "Route 66" and Mel had to take me to Doctor Kildare because I was dying of the curse. Dr Gillespie was called in. He took it seriously even if Mum didn't. I nearly died in the car in Dr Kildare's arms. Then Maggie came out on her way to the sweet shop and she laughed again and said it didn't look like dying to her. But she promised not to tell anyway. When she came back she'd bought a bottle of Tizer, which she offered to share. She wouldn't have done that if I hadn't been cursed, I can tell you.

So everyone was very nice, in the end, and didn't act a

160

bit like they wished I'd never been born. Even Dad when he got home, stroked my hair and asked me if I felt all right and I could tell that Mum had told him because he mumbled and went a bit red. He always did that when he was embarrassed. Girl's things phased him a bit because he only had brothers. Three of them. No sisters. Some people have all the luck.

Mum had made my favourite cold dinner, Scotch eggs and salad with lots of salad cream and a treacle tart for afters. She made it in the hot oven. In this heat. Just for me. We had whipped cream and she let me lick the spoon - the big serving one - for a special treat. So everyone was really lovely in the end. Except Julie. She didn't say anything to me when she got home. Nothing at all, even when Mum told her. She was still cross and I decided that she could get on with it.

I decided she was the ungrateful one. I had tried to protect her and save her from Lockheart and I had got her and David back together again because without me they'd still be crying by the practice wall, but if she couldn't see that, she could get knotted. She was such a cow. But I hoped she wouldn't turn David against me because he was a lovely person and a true friend. Unlike her.

* * * * * *

The next day I put in my claim for a dog. I decided I was giving up on sisters. Mum and Dad had been talking the night before as they walked round the garden planning the next daisy massacre, and I was in the rockery discovering new worlds despite my infirmity, and I overheard them talking about "cashing in" and "capitalising on the situation when the time was right", so I wondered if I should too. You know, cash in on the sympathy from being cursed.

I had decided that what I wanted most in life was a dog.

161

Or better still, two dogs. Dalmatians, of course, because they're the best. They are ancient carriage dogs and used to journeys and could come with me on "Route 66." But if there were no Dalmatians available, then a Red Setter like Rusty because they are so beautiful. Dogs are man's best friend. Unlike sisters, they are loyal and kind and incredibly devoted. And all they want in exchange is a good walk and a few smelly biscuits.

So I figured that if I had my dogs, I could put the man business on hold because I would never get anywhere near David now that Julie had decided I was Enemy Number One. And I had a tummy ache and a spot on my nose and I was all swaddled up with this pad thing, so I wasn't glamorous or sexy at all, and I wasn't likely to be ever, as far as I could tell. It was hopeless. All my efforts to find a man who would adore me had only resulted in my finding a man I could adore, who was my sister's boyfriend. Bit of an own goal, really. So I decided a dog was the answer. To be my constant companion and my one true love. Because he wouldn't have a wife who was having a baby or a girlfriend who was my sister.

I had reasoned it all out and I put it to Mum and Dad. It was going to be brilliant. They would never have to worry about me in the park ever again because my dogs would protect me to the death. Dogs do that. Always. It's a known fact.

I told them it was going to be absolutely perfect. Except it wasn't because Mum said no. No, no. no. She didn't want a dog (she wouldn't even consider two), who would be a nine day wonder and who would end up looking after him and taking him for walks in all weathers while I was at school? Who would have to train him and stop him from eating all our shoes and being sick on the carpet and leaving his doggy hairs all over the sofa? To say nothing of what he would leave on the lawn. She was horrible. I didn't realise there were so many ways of saying no. I tried to make her see reason, but Dad said if that was how Mum felt, that was the end of it. So I had to give up. But I got my parting shot in.

As I was going up to bed and out of clip round the ear

162

range, I muttered, "You really ought to have a dog, Mum. Because Nazis always do. Hitler's was called "Blondie."

Mum didn't hear me. She was talking to Maggie. Dad did. He followed me out of the room.

"I had no idea you were so well informed, Sally. Perhaps your expensive education has paid off at last." He was very sarcastic. He didn't like anyone being horrible to Mum.

"Why are you suddenly so keen on having a dog?"

He was actually grinning Making fun of me. I hated him.

"Because I'm always in the doghouse here, so if I had a dog, I wouldn't be alone."

He laughed and patted my hand. It was on the bannister. I took it off. I didn't want him patting me. I hated him. I hated them all. He smiled at me.

"Go to bed, child. Stop bellyaching."

How could I? I was cursed and it hurt like hell.

* * * * * *

It was so hot that night I thought I was going to die. The whole of my stomach and back ached with the most awful pain. It felt like I was being split in two. The pad was hot and sticky and there was no chance at all of Julie's fan. She'd have rather I'd died than show me any mercy.

I woke up in the middle of a nightmare. Tim was winding me up in a beautiful silken sari, like Princess Julie in our play. I looked gorgeous. Only he was pulling it tighter and tighter and then he looked at me like he had by the tree and he said, "You must never tell anyone, Sally", and I was wound up so tightly I couldn't move. There were voices shouting in the park and I tried to call out to them but I couldn't breathe. I woke up gasping for breath and I was all twisted up in the sheet, so I untangled myself and slowly the room took shape in the

163

darkness. Then I realised I could still hear the voices. They were coming from outside.

"Bitch!" The voice was very loud. It was followed by the sound of breaking glass. Then the screaming started. Mum and Dad's door opened and Dad went downstairs. I ran along the corridor to Mum. I met Julie on the way. She was so pale, even her lips looked white. And all the time the screaming went on.

"You filthy little scrubber! Get out here!"

I stopped at the top of the stairs and looked down. Someone had thrown a brick though our front door. It was lying on the carpet surrounded by broken glass. I went into the spare room and looked out of the window. Two women were standing by the street lamp outside our house. One of them was the Battleaxe, screaming her head off. In the orange glare, her face was so twisted up that it looked all mouth. Her eyes had almost disappeared. Standing beside her was Jeannie. She was screaming too.

"Give me back my husband, bitch!" She looked ghastly, monstrous. A tiny head on an abdomen so swollen and distended, it seemed about to burst.

I watched Dad go outside in his pyjamas.

"What the hell's going on? Who are you?"

That seemed to make the Battleaxe even madder. "Ask your precious daughter who we are!"

Jeannie started to cry. Loudly. All gulps and hiccups. The Battleaxe screamed on. A constant stream of hatefulness. Even when her voice cracked with so much screaming, she didn't stop.

"I have no idea what this is about."

"Don't give me that! Don't you play the innocent with me!"

Dad looked completely bewildered. The Battleaxe went on.

"You tell that scabby little tart to stop fucking my son-in-law."

She tried to stand up straight, but she was swaying about and had to hold on to the lamp post. "And my Jeannie about to

164

have a baby any minute."

"I can see that. Now look, calm down and tell me what this is about."

The screaming started up again. "If you don't stop this, I'll call the police." He didn't know what to do. You could tell from his voice. Every time he tried to reason with her it only made things worse.

"That's right! You call the police, you bastard. Go on then! Let's tell them all about David and my Jeannie and your cunt of a daughter who can't keep her legs closed!"

"That's enough!" He was angry now. He walked back into the house.

But I could already hear the phone dial turning. Someone was calling the police from upstairs. Maggie. He called up to us.

" I don't want any of you coming downstairs, do you hear me? There's broken glass everywhere."

Maggie walked out of their bedroom to the top of the stairs.

"I've already called the police, Dad." Her voice was calm, but her legs were shaking.

"Good girl." Then he went into his study and shut the door. The screaming stopped. I could hear Mum and Julie talking in low voices. They were in Mum's room, but they had shut the door. Maggie came into the spare room. I was still staring out of the window. She came over to join me. After a few minutes the police arrived. They parked in our drive with their blue light flashing. When the Battleaxe and Jeannie saw them coming, they tried to walk away, but Jeannie was still crying and her mother couldn't walk straight. Two policemen got out of the car and went to talk to them. One of them wrote something down in a little pad.

Then Dad opened the door and the police came in. Mum went down in her dressing gown. We could hear them talking. I turned to Maggie, but I couldn't say anything. She said, "We'd better go back to bed." She followed me out of the room. "You've leaked." I didn't know what she meant. "You've got blood on your nightie."

She took me into the bathroom and helped me clean up. Then she gave me one of her nighties to wear. We got into her bed. I didn't want to be on my own.

After a while the police left. We heard the front door close. Then Mum and Dad started to clear up the broken glass. It took them ages. Then we heard them go into the kitchen. We couldn't sleep. We went to see if Julie was okay but she had locked her door and when we asked her, she didn't answer. So we went back to Maggie's bed. In the end we fell asleep.

* * * * * *

When Mags and I went down the next morning, they were already in the study. We could hear them talking. The broken glass had been cleared away, but there was a hole in the door where the glass had been. Dad had taped some cardboard over it.

We went into the kitchen. The tea things were still on the table. But no food. It seemed we weren't having any breakfast. No table laid, no butter or jam put out, no cereal packets on the counter. Nothing. It wasn't like a normal morning at all. Maggie poured us both a glass of milk and got the biscuit tin down. She was very practical, Maggie. Good in a crisis.

"Good job we already know, eh Sall? Because no-one ever tells us anything."

"They don't have to. We already know more than they do, anyway." She looked at me and laughed. "You do, Sherlock. You've known all along. "

Then she took another biscuit and pushed the tin over to me. She looked at me hard as she ate her biscuit.

"You know, in spite of your many blunders, you're not as daft as you look, are you?" And I felt better then, because with Maggie, that was about as good as it got.

166

But I didn't feel better for long because I was worried about the other one. Even if she had been a cow. The one who was locked up in the study with Mum and Dad. The one whose occasional wails we could hear three rooms away. And then there was David. What had happened to him? Where was he now?

It was a while before I found out.

CHAPTER 13

Mum and Dad were appalled. Mum told Julie that she was "hurt and disgusted", not just by her having an affair with a married man, and one whose wife was about to give birth, but because she hadn't felt she could confide in her mother. The one person she could always trust. And that she had put them "in the position of having to find out from a drunken fishwife and a brick through the front door".

They had her holed up in the study for hours, but they forgot to close the door, so when Mags and I went into the hall to look at the damage from close to, we could hear everything. Mum spoke first and then Dad told Julie in a quiet, steady voice that he hoped she realised that she had brought the family name about as low as it could get. She started to cry then. It was very hard for her. Because not only did she have to cope with a drunken maniac who wanted to kill her, but now her name was mud with her parents. She wasn't used to that. She'd been perfect before.

She walked out of the study crying in her baby dolls. She was so upset she didn't even go mad when she saw Mags and I were listening. And she seemed to have forgotten all about the stockings. That showed you how upset she was. When she passed me she said, "It's over now, Sall. They've told me to make my choice. It's either David or them." And I started to cry too then because I knew they meant it. So I followed her upstairs, but not into her room. And Maggie came up too. Because we were the younger generation and we had to stick

169

together. Even if we couldn't talk.

We didn't come down all morning. We just stayed, each in our separate rooms, silent and miserable. Just going over in our minds what had happened. I was thinking about David, too. I wondered if he was crying as well. At about eleven o'clock Maggie went downstairs. A few minutes later she came back with some glasses, a jug of Ribena and the biscuit tin on a tray. She wasn't going to let us starve. Even if our hearts were breaking. She knocked on Julie's door. I went with her.

"Go away."

"No. You've got to have a drink or you'll be ill."

The door opened. We went in and Maggie poured out the Ribena. Julie drank it all down in one go. It's thirsty work all that crying. I couldn't bear it.

"Will you be all right? Because it was our secret and I ..."

I had failed her utterly. Both of them. I had loved them both so much and tried my very best, but the mission had been a complete flop. I had failed to protect either of them. I must have looked a bit tormented because Julie looked at both of us and then smiled with her tear-stained face all twisted up and funny.

"You two ...old Florence Nightingale and Madame Parker." She shook her head.

"Come on into the morgue." And she walked back across the room. Then she sat down in her armchair, with her legs all drawn up as if she had tummy ache.

We didn't know what to say. Julie was in a pain that we couldn't understand. It was beyond us. So we didn't say anything. We drank our drinks and Maggie pushed the biscuit tin towards Julie, but she wouldn't eat anything. So we all sat for a while together and then we left her, and went to get washed and dressed. After a bit, we went downstairs.

The atmosphere there was terrible. Mum and Dad looked grim. They barely spoke, even to each other. They walked around the house with their mouths shut in a thin, tight line. No-one went to work that day. Mel was supposed to come over, but

170

I cancelled her. I said I was ill. I couldn't talk to anyone. Not even her.

Later that morning a man came to repair the door. He did it really quickly. It seemed repairing us would be more difficult.

The whole family was in shock. And in the days that followed, it didn't get any better. We weren't used to being attacked. Mum and Dad tried to appear as if they were on top of the situation, as if things were "Under control". But you only had to look at them to see that they weren't. They both looked very tired. Dad had big black hoops under his eyes and in the night you could hear him walking around the house. He seemed to spend most of the time in his study now. And Mum suddenly looked older. Lines appeared around her eyes and mouth like a fine spiders web that had not been there before. Julie crept around the house like a little mouse. She went to work and then came home. She never went out. There was never any sign of David.

The police came back and talked to Dad. They had interviewed the Battleaxe and Jeannie and warned them to keep away from us. They wanted to know if Dad was pressing charges. He had said no, he told us. Because enough damage had been done and he wanted to stop it right there. To prevent his daughters' name being dragged through the mud. He looked disgusted when he said that, as if the words tasted foul. Julie just got more and more quiet. She was sick a lot. I asked her if she was ill and she said it was "just nerves". Well, why wouldn't she have nerves ? She wasn't used to people wanting to kill her. I was furious with Lockheart. Where had he been when we needed him? I decided I wasn't going to watch "No Hiding Place" anymore. Because he was just a big sham. With his screeching car and silly hat. Useless.

David just disappeared from our lives. No more seeing him walking down the road every morning, smiling and happy, on his way to meet Julie, or in the evenings watching them kiss in the park. He just vanished. As if we had never known him. And at the same time, Julie seemed to shrink before our eyes.

171

She still looked nice, she couldn't help that, but all her glamour, her bright colours and gloss, everything that made you want to look at her, seemed to have evaporated. It just disappeared like morning mist

Suddenly, she had this quiet little life. And it was strange because just as Mum and Dad seemed older, she seemed younger. The whole bright adventure of her life had petered out.

I talked about it a lot to Maggie. Perhaps she could find a cure? A solution? She was good at that. Because things as they were were awful. No David and Julie turning into a ghost before she had even died.

"Can't she ever see him again?" Who was I asking for? Her or me?

Mags shook her head. "No. They wouldn't have it. They couldn't now, could they?"

"Why not? What ever happened to True Love Winning Through, you know "Amor whatsit omnia."

Maggie screwed up her face. She always took Latin very seriously. "Well, it was doomed from the start, really, wasn't it?"

"Why?" I didn't want it to be doomed. I wanted my sister back, bright and sexy and different. And I wanted David back too. More than anything.

"Because you're only s'posed to have One True Love and David's had two."

"Julie hasn't."

" I know. It stinks. It's totally unfair. I'm really worried about her, Sall. She looks awful and she's always being sick." So she had noticed too. She sucked the end of her pencil and got that cross eyed look Maggie gets on the rare occasion that a problem defeats her. You could tell she was worrying and Mags didn't do that often. She didn't have to. Most problems were a breeze to her.

I gave it a lot of thought. Julie was as miserable as sin. You only had to look at her to see that. She was quiet and dull. She had never been like this before. I longed for her to howl and scream. She'd never been like other people. She spent most of

172

her life dancing on ice in a fairy tale, for God's sake. She couldn't just come back and be ordinary in Northwick Circle.

I didn't want her to be ordinary. Except now she was. She slunk about the place, looking beaten, like those poor old dogs the RSPCA rescue. It was terrible. Love wasn't supposed to be like this. It's supposed to be about roses and kisses and happy ever after. It's not supposed to end up with everyone being like a stray dog for the rest of their lives.

* * * * * *

One morning soon after that I went in to see Julie when she was dressing to go to work. Except she wasn't. She was just sitting there in the armchair, staring at the window. But she couldn't see out because the curtains were still drawn. That did it. I went back to my room and got something. Something we were going to need. Because I was going to tackle this situation. It was getting desperate. Dad wandered round the house all night like a werewolf and Mum looked a thousand years old. Julie had almost stopped speaking entirely. Even Maggie was worried. We had to put a stop to this before we became Herbert Lom's patients in "The Human Jungle."

Julie just sat there looking blank and a bit barmy. She looked terrible. Beneath her tan her skin had a horrid green tinge and she looked more tired than she had when she had gone to bed the night before. She was still wearing her nightie. Her nose was shiny and her hair was dirty. Things were running backwards in this house. She looked up when I came in and then went back to staring at the closed curtains.

I knew exactly what I had to do. I had figured it all out first thing this morning. My curse had finished and my head was clear. I would just have to be very brave. Captain Cook and Clive of India never got anywhere by dodging the issue. They marched straight in to sticky situations and grasped the nettle.

173

So would I.

"You're very unhappy. Don't argue, I can tell." I sat down on the bed. She hadn't made it yet.

"All right, Sherlock. You got me. Now what?" She sounded as if she didn't much care.

"Well, we can't go on like this. This family's falling apart. You've got a broken heart and the Battleaxe might murder David. I wouldn't put it past her. She's a very nasty piece of work."

"I'm with you there, Sall." I was going to have to help her. She wasn't going to figure this one out for herself. I wasn't even sure she was listening. Obviously, the whole thing was beyond her. But not me. I was back on form and on the case.

"I've figured it all out. It wasn't easy, but I've cracked it. It's like this. Mum and Dad are going to be cross anyway. Because you're not perfect. But, in the end, they'll come round. Because we're not perfect either. They still love us. I mean, even Maggie's never won a cup on Sports Day, has she? See what I mean?"

She nodded. "Go on." Did the ghost of a smile cross her face? At any rate, she was listening now.

"Now look, Jeannie will always be unhappy with David because at the time she needed him to love her most, he didn't. He loved you instead. So they'll never be happy. It's a lost cause. Thus, in conclusion, one lot will come round and the other's hopeless. So we can forget about both of them. Do you follow?"

This was good. I was sounding like Miss Riley. That must mean that I was right because she always was and Julie had that bewildered, slightly panicky look that always comes over Mel in the algebra class.

"Right. The rest is simple. You and David are here and you are miserable. You are miserable because you are here. QED. Among the Mums and Dads and the Battleaxes. To say nothing of the Jeannie. And we've established that's a lost cause. But, if you were not here, if you were far away from all of them, you and David could be happy because you love each

174

other. So, you can be salvaged. You'll have to go. To the South Seas or somewhere. We'll have to smuggle you out in the dead of night."

Julie still looked completely mystified. "You know, like kegs of brandy." What was the matter with her? She'd read "Jamaica Inn."

"So", I had brought my money tin with me for the purpose. I paused here because I was about to make the most unselfish gesture of my entire life and I wanted her to mark the moment.

Then I emptied the tin, both compartments, out onto the bed. It was my most secret stash and NOBODY, not even Mel, knew about it. It was for emergencies only. In case I needed to leave the country in a hurry or buy a present for Mum, whose birthday was coming up in August. I had wanted to surprise her with an extra bottle of "Blue Grass" , the only one ever not bought by Dad at Christmas. I'd imagined how she would hug me and tell me I was the best daughter in the whole wide world with her eyes full of tears. Oh well, never mind. We'd had enough tears in this family.

Then I came back to the present. "You have got your passport, haven't you?" She wouldn't get very far without it. Dad kept all of ours locked up in his desk. If Julie's was in there too, we were sunk. You'd never get it out without taking an axe to that desk. And if you did that you'd better go away and never come back because if you stayed you wouldn't sit down again. Ever. Dad would make sure of that.

But Julie was nodding. "Yeah, I always keep my own passport. For when I'm on tour. It's in that drawer somewhere." She waved vaguely towards her dressing table. Once reassured, I moved on swiftly. I started to count the money. I knew roughly what I had but I wanted to make the point. It took me a while because it was mostly in sixpences and threepenny bits, with only a few half crowns. And it's very difficult to pile up money on a bed that's all creased up and rumpled.

So I had to begin again twice. But in the end it was all

counted, and I laid it out as best I could with the Gary Millar photo I had cut out from the paper and the beautiful little black cat with diamond eyes that I got in a cracker at Christmas. It was for luck and I loved it. Oh well, she'd better have that too. She was going to need it.

Julie was getting restless. "Sally, what is all this about?" She still hadn't twigged.

"You, stupid. It's for you. The whole lot. 15/11d. Go on. Take it. "nd the cat." I was being very generous. It was all the money I had in the world. And Mum's birthday was only three weeks away.

"But what's it for?" Oh dear. She didn't used to be this thick.

"You. You and David. To get you away to the South Seas. Where you can be happy because love is all you need and amor thingy whatsit. You know. Where you can be happy in the sun and dive for pearls and eat breadfruit with the natives. Like Fletcher Christian."

She really did have a wonderful sister. Perhaps I could have the cat back because she was lucky enough, having me.

But she just sat there, smiling that twisty sort of smile that didn't reach her eyes. She looked crazy. In dire need of Herbert Lom. Then she laughed. At first it was a horrid creaky laugh that sounded like a rusty hinge and then it caught in her throat. Then she began howling out loud.

I just stood there. I didn't know what to do. She held out her arms, but she couldn't have seen me because her eyes were all screwed up and a downpour was running out of them. So I hugged her hard. I wanted to shut her up quick before someone heard her and carted her off to the loony bin, carrying on like that. I held her very tightly, and she calmed down and began to cry like a normal person. But still great gulping sobs that sounded as if she was going to be sick, and I was a bit worried about that because I was hugging her. But she wouldn't let me go, she just clung on as if we were both drowning. So I clung back and I thought how odd it was because, although she was all

176

grown up and had the big bosoms and long legs, her shoulders were quite narrow and her wrists were as small as mine. She just cried and cried. I thought she'd never stop. She was like an animal whose owner had left it behind, who couldn't even begin to think of a life without him.

I held her until she'd stopped crying, got passed the hiccup stage and blown her nose. Then she looked up and said,

"I can't go, Sal. I'd love to, but I can't because he won't go with me. I asked him. I went to see him at his office and I begged him to come away with me. But he said no. He's sticking by Jeannie because he can't abandon the baby. But he said he doesn't love her. He said he loves me and he always will, but she got so upset that night she had to go to hospital. They were afraid she'd lose the baby."

And then her head flopped back with her hair all sticking up in lacquered clumps, and her eyes all wild and witchy and she started laughing that crazy laugh again. I shook her. "Stop it." I shook her again. Hard. She stopped and looked at me "Do you want to know what's funny?" No I didn't. I couldn't imagine anything in the least bit funny about any of it.

"What's really funny is that he is."

I shook her again. I had a this horrible feeling that something was spreading across our lives like an ink stain that would never wash out.

"What are you talking about?"

She blew all the air out of her mouth in one go, then bit her bottom lip.

"I'm pregnant, Sal. I had the test on Monday. And I'm going to have to kill my baby because he won't leave hers."

I stared at her in absolute horror. Because just when I'd thought I had the solution she had revealed something that was far worse than anything I could have imagined.

I dropped my arms. I didn't want to hug her now. I didn't want to be near her. Or the other thing. Because it wasn't just her now. Someone else growing inside her. It was horrible. I ran out of the room and downstairs. I left her and her secret and her

177

craziness and all my money. I went out into the garden and ran up the rockery, gulping in the fresh air. I wanted to get away. As far away as I could. Because none of it made any sense. It didn't make sense at all.

* * * * *

That was where Maggie found me hours later. Sitting red and burning in the bright noon sun in my imaginary boat, trying to put myself somewhere else. To imagine myself anywhere as long as it wasn't here. In Florence Nightingale's darkened ward or on Captain Cook's endless horizon, trying make other worlds my own. Anything except this one. A world turned upside down. A world I had been told ran on certain lines, that suddenly didn't. A world of nonsense and pain, where adults screamed like banshees and hurled bricks through windows and a baby not yet born would have to be killed because another one would be born first. And those who loved were torn apart and those who didn't were chained together like convicts. Why? I kept trying to understand. I failed.

I didn't see her come into the garden. I only noticed her when she stood at the base of the rockery.

"Get out of the sun. You're burning." It was true - my shoulders had begun to sting.

"What's up, fishface?" I couldn't speak. She climbed up the rockery and sat down beside me.

"Budge up. It's Julie, right?" I nodded, dumb with misery.

She looked ahead bleakly. "She's pregnant, isn't she?"

"Yes."

"Oh God." We sat together without talking. We let it sink in. Then Maggie stood up. "Come on."

"Where we going?"

178

"Inside before you get third degree burns. You look like a lobster, Sally. It looks as if it hurts."

It did, but I didn't care. I shrugged. "What now?"

"We're going to talk to Julie. She didn't go to work today. She was too busy being sick. I could hear her." She was already climbing briskly down the rockery. I followed her.

"What did Mum say?"

"Nothing. They're barely talking, hadn't you noticed? She stuck her head round Mum's bedroom door, announced she had a "Migraine" and then locked herself back in the morgue. We've got to sort her out, Sall, before she goes off her rocker."

You couldn't argue with that. Not if you'd seen what I had. We marched indoors like the Earp brothers entering the OK Coral.

I hadn't a clue what Maggie thought we were going to say. But clearly she did and, as she was the only one who hadn't gone bonkers, she seemed worth following. So I did.

We knocked at Julie's door and waited til she let us in. She didn't look pleased to see us. Still in her old nightie, with yesterday's mascara all smudged round her eyes and her hair unbrushed, she frightened me. I didn't like this crazy new sister who laughed and cried and made them both sound the same. She plonked herself down in the armchair and went back to staring at her curtains.

Maggie sat on the bed facing her. "You'll have to tell Mum, Julie." Her tone was gentle but firm.

"She's told you then." It wasn't a question.

"She didn't have to. It's obvious. And you'll have to tell Mum before she cottons on."

Julie reached into her bag and pulled out a cigarette. Then she struck a match and lit it and put the stick down in the overflowing ashtray by her chair. It was disgusting. Full of old cigarette buts and tons of ash all mixed up with sweet wrappers and a rusty hairpin.

"Well, Maggie, in case you haven't noticed Mummy and I aren't exactly on good terms just at the moment. I can't play "cuddle up and tell Mummy " because she hates my guts right now."

Her voice was bitter and sarcastic and yes, downright nasty. Then she blew smoke in Maggie's face. I was beginning to hate her. But Mags would allow no such distractions. Coolly, she replied,

"Rubbish. She adores you. Any fool can see that. You've just hurt her, that's all. She thinks you've behaved like an idiot. I wonder why?" Game, set and match. Julie looked as if she were going to hit her.

"So what are you going to do - tell her?"

"No. You are. What else can you do?"

Julie looked round the room as if she might find the answer there. In fact, she looked everywhere except at us.

"Oh... I 've got friends who'll help me out. Friends who know the score. All you need's a little cash. Oldest story in the world. Happens all the time." She was back with the show bizz voice, brittle and drawling, but the hand that held the cigarette trembled. Maggie took control. Her voice was crisp and determined.

"You're not having a back street abortion, Julie. You can bleed to death. That happens all the time too."

She'd won and they both knew it. But Julie wasn't running up the white flag yet.

"What do you suggest I do, Maggie? Give you your first lesson in Obstetrics? Move in with Jeannie and form a harem?" But her voice was wobbly and the questions sounded less like anger than a cry for help.

"No. I suggest you tell Mum. Because she'll find a doctor who won't kill you. Your survival matters to me somehow. God knows why."

She had cast iron guts, that girl. Then she threw in her trump card. "I'll go with you if you like."

And suddenly Julie was biting her lip and nodding her head. Maggie was fabulous. She would not let Julie wreck her life. Every time Julie began to do a number and wander off,

180

Maggie dragged her back. She was magnificent. This was what her brains were for. She could pull people out of despair with them. She could keep thinking when everyone else could only feel.

Then she went downstairs and came back with Mum. I took the dressing table stool into the corner of the room and sat there quietly. Mum and Maggie sat down on the bed, Julie was still parked in her armchair.

Maggie started talking first. Simply, in a calm, quiet voice, she told Mum the facts.

"Oh my God, Julie, no!" Mum was like Julie and me. She was a wailer.

Maggie cut her off straight away. "No use crying over spilt milk, Mum. It's done now. All we can do is deal with it." You couldn't argue with her. She was the only thing that was making sense.

"It's a practical problem with a practical solution. The less hysterics we have now the better we deal with it."

I told you. Magnificent. Her freckly old face intent with thinking and her own weird brand of kindness. She took charge completely and Mum let her. She asked Mum to find someone who would help Julie. Because proper practical help was what was needed now. Not shouting and "hysterics". She said we'd had enough of that the other night. That was clever. Mum would have rather died than behave like the Battleaxe. Whatever the circumstances. After Maggie said that, there wasn't a wail out of her. She listened and thought about it. Then she spoke and although her voice did wobble a bit, she coped.

"Julie, I don't approve of this. I don't approve at all. But Maggie is right. It's done now and we must deal with it. I'll speak to Aunty Eileen. She'll know someone. And if she doesn't, she'll know someone who does. And she'll keep quiet. I'll ring her right now. No, I won't. I'll go and see her."

She was probably dying for a jolly good cry. The one Maggie wouldn't allow her. On Aunty Eileen's shoulder.

Aunty Eileen was Mum's cousin. She was a District

181

Nurse and she lived near us in Preston Road. She was very nice. Capable, brisk and kind, only like Maggie, she didn't like being caught at it. She didn't like displays either. And I was very happy when Mum said all this because it meant she was being Mum again. She would deal with it now. All she had needed was a terrific kick in the right direction. And that she had got from Maggie.

Then Mum stood up. "We'll sort this out, Julie. And we'll get through it. Somehow." She was a bit rocky there for a second, but she made for the door. Then she turned round and looked at the three of us. "The only good thing to come out of this whole dreadful business is the way you three have stuck together. Don't think I haven't noticed. It's the only thing that's kept me going. In all this mess, if you three can stick together like this, we can't have got it all wrong." That was almost a wail.

Grown ups are very odd. They always trace everything back to themselves. This had nothing to do with them. Perhaps that's what they found so hard to take.

"And as for you, Margaret," she looked at her quite sternly, "when did you become so wise?" Maggie squirmed. She hated this sort of thing.

She went all red and stared down at her feet as if finding them there was a surprise. Then she mumbled, "I'm not really wise, Mum. I'm just not a Romantic. I'm like Dad."

"Oh my God, your father! What am I going to tell him? This will kill him." That was a wail. Good and proper.

But nothing phased old Miss Frigidaire. "Then don't tell him. I shan't." I was so shocked, I laughed. But Mum just nodded and swallowed it whole without a murmur.

That was how Maggie saved the whole family. And she wasn't even on a mission. Although perhaps she had her own mission. To stop people wrecking their lives. That looked like becoming a lifelong crusade. But for the moment, she had saved us. All of us.

182

* * * * * *

Later, Maggie told me what exactly what an abortion was. It made me feel sick.

I took refuge in the park a lot after that. With Mel, of course. In the end, I told her. Well, not in the end, in the beginning actually. In fact, the first time I saw her. Well, she was my best friend.

She didn't say much. She just listened. Like her mother. And then she sort of squeezed my hand to show that she understood and gave me two Rolos. In one go. She was normally a bit stingy with her Rolos.

Mum tried not to tell Dad, like Maggie had said. It was a good idea, but it couldn't be done. Dad could always tell if something was being kept from him. Mum didn't stand a chance because she and Julie were so miserable it was like a fog that got in everywhere, however much they tried to keep it out. If you shut the door on it, it just wafted in underneath.

Mum had gone to see Aunty Eileen straight away. She came back red eyed and resolute. After three days and a lot of phone calls, she took Julie to see a doctor. The two of them came back from that silent and soaked in misery. With a determination to carry on that was even worse than the misery. Mum boiled the potatoes dry that night. The saucepan was ruined and the kitchen smelled of burning. We had to have bread and butter with our chops instead.

Julie left the bath running and nearly flooded the whole house. They were like a pair of zombies, really. The living dead.

You didn't have to be very clever to work out that something was horribly wrong. And Dad was clever. It took him about two seconds to get it out of Mum. And when he had , his silence, and the way he looked sad and angry and helpless all at once was worse than their tears. You could see it tearing him apart. So it was very good to get away because the atmosphere at home was so awful, it choked you. You had to get out to breathe. In the park, under the trees, the shade was cool and Mel and I could have our play and be anything we wanted. Away from their agony. Which was the most terrific relief.

Mum was not on patrol much now. She asked a lot less questions than before because she was so preoccupied with Julie. I think she reckoned that if I was with Mel, Mel's Mum would keep tabs on us. And normally, she would have. But she couldn't now because she was away. Maddy had had her appendix out and Mel's Mum had taken her to Jersey to recover or something. So there were no tabs on us because Aunty Peggy couldn't have kept tabs on anyone if she'd tried. So she just didn't bother and we were free agents. It was brilliant.

The park became our second home. We took sanctuary in it like Thomas a Becket and the knights of old.

We met up with Tim and Rusty for the first time since the stocking fiasco. They were waiting for us with the fruit gums just like always. Tim had kept his promise. He had bought the stockings for us - all four pairs of "American Tan" - two for Julie and two for us. I didn't know what to say at first. And then when he kept asking I had to tell him. I told him that the rescue had come too late. Because just about everything that could have gone wrong had. It wasn't his fault. He had kept his promise and been a true friend and I couldn't say anymore because I was trying not to cry. He was terribly nice. He put his arm round me and said he was very sorry to hear that, but he had bought the stockings anyway and he hoped that one day we would wear them just for him. So I said that we would.

After that Mel and I met every morning halfway round the circle and went on together to the park. We wore shorts and plimsolls, so falling off the stepping stones was not a problem. Our shorts were too short to get wet and we tied the laces together and wore our shoes round our necks. Only our feet got wet and they soon dried.

We learned to put our purses in our pockets but never a
184

chocolate bar, because they melted. Apples were okay so we took them too. Oranges were brilliant because of the juice. And fruit was free. We bought cold drinks from the chip shop and had fresh chips for lunch. It was perfect. No-one worried where we were until tea time and by then we were home.

We started a new game. Mel was reading a book called "The Scarlet Pimpernel". A Baroness wrote it and it was thrilling. The Scarlet Pimpernel was a bit like Simon Templar only in history. He was a sort of secret agent who seemed really dim, but he rescued French aristocrats from the jaws of death. Because the rabble wanted to behead them all.

It was excellent. We could use all the skills we had learned watching Julie and David to spring Madame la Marquise from the Bastille. If only we could get her wig off. French lords and ladies were very fond of these big white wigs. I don't know why because they were full of fleas, but they were a dead giveaway because the rabble couldn't afford them. Mel knew all about it. She had seen paintings of them in some palace in France. She said you could see everything in these pictures. I asked her if she could see the fleas too, but she shut me up. She was a bit serious about history. Her parents were too. I mean imagine having to spend your holidays looking at pictures of dead people. Even when it's not raining. They like that kind of thing. I prefer the beach myself.

Anyway, it was a jolly good game. We bowed and curtsied and we danced something called a minuet (well, our idea of it, which was a sort of slow and stately jive). Tim and Rusty joined in when they were there and that was always a hoot because Tim couldn't dance to save his life and Rusty just jumped about.

Tim was a lovely grown up to play with because he just joined in with everything. He didn't mind if it was daft. We went to balls in great houses and spirited the victims out from under the very nose of the fiendish Chauvelin. He was the villain. He wanted to execute everybody. I rather liked him.

We loved the Scarlet Pimpernel. His name was Sir Percy

Blakeney and at first you think he's a real twit who keeps falling asleep all over the place. But he turns out to be incredibly clever in the end. We took it in turns to be him. His wife was really chronic, she was called Marguerite. She was a great beauty and a complete dead loss . No one wanted to be her. Her brother Armand was almost as bad. Sir Percy himself nearly got killed trying to rescue him. I wouldn't have bothered. Sometimes I thought old Chauvelin had the right idea.

Tim did ask us again if we would wear the stockings just for him, but it was so hot that we wore shorts all the time, so we told him that we would when it got cooler and became skirt time again. He seemed quite happy with that.

* * * * * *

I still missed David. I thought about him all the time and I wondered how he was. I couldn't imagine him stuck with Jeannie and the Battleaxe for the rest of his life. It seemed such a terrible waste. He was full of love and jokes and his own brand of craziness He could make the most ordinary things seem special - like Mrs Fisher's tulip. I couldn't face peardrops any more. I missed his too loud laugh, his skinny legs in their drainpipe trousers, his huge feet on the end of them in their daft pointy shoes, and his hairdo that never stayed in place like Efram Zimbalist Jnrs' did. His smile when he saw Julie coming to meet him. The look on his face before he kissed her. I would miss that for the rest of my life.

In the meantime, we immersed ourselves in the park and the French Revolution because frankly, it was a lot more cheerful than what was going on at home.

Aunty Eileen had found a clinic. It was in Surrey. Julie had to stay in overnight and Mum got herself a room in a B & B nearby "in case". In case what she didn't say.

That morning Julie came down with her white make up bag all packed. She wore her second best dress - it was made of shiny white cotton with little cherries printed on it and it had a red leather belt. She looked terrified. Mum looked determined - to see this thing through. She was brisk and business like and hardly looked at Julie. Or me. But when she said goodbye, she hugged Maggie tight and whispered "Don't you ever do this to me." And Mags, wriggled out of the hug, and said "I won't," quite fiercely.

Finally Mum turned to me, but she was still talking to Maggie, "You'll look after Sally, won't you?" Honestly, as if I was five years old. Then she fussed about the kitchen telling us what we were to have for supper and how she had put it all out in the fridge ready, it was all cold and all Maggie had to do was lay the table. Dad would be back at the normal time. She didn't speak to me at all. I seemed to have become invisible. So I pulled a face at Julie who was just standing there with her bag and she almost smiled, but couldn't quite manage it. Then Mum picked up her handbag and little overnight case and gave me the briefest of kisses, a sort of peck really, and said she'd be back soon and Dad and Maggie would look after me.

Julie followed Mum down the path to the car and she looked so scared and alone, I ran up and hugged her. And I said, "You don't have to go. If you don't want to." She almost cracked then. She stood stock still for a moment and then brushed my hair out of my eyes and said, "Yes, I do, Madame Parker," very softly. She winked at me, but a tear ran out of her eye and down her cheek. And I hugged her tight. I didn't want her to go away and be hurt because I knew this was something that would hurt for the rest of her life. It wouldn't be over when she came back. I felt that today I was the only person who was actually seeing Julie. Not the situation or it's solution, but her. This whole hurting person. She let me hug her and then she prised me off and tried to smile. And I lost it completely and I cried. Standing there like a complete nana in the drive. I knew we weren't just

187

losing a baby no-one wanted. We were losing my sister. Then they drove away. Maggie took me back into the house.

For the first time in weeks, it was cloudy. It kept trying to rain but not managing. A few heavy drops fell and then it stopped. It was stuffy and airless. A horrible day.

Dad got back on time, but he was very quiet. We all were. Maggie and I put the supper out and we did it very carefully, arranging the plates of ham and bread and butter and salad so it looked nice for him. But he didn't seem to notice. He could have been eating breezeblocks for all he cared.

I tried to make conversation, but it's a bit difficult with only one. The conversation tends to run dry. Dad had poured himself a big glass of whisky and he brought it to the table. He didn't usually do that. He and Mum had their drinks together first. But it looked quite nice in it's crystal glass, all golden and amber. So I tried to talk about wine and how the French drink that and not whisky, but that didn't last long because I don't know anything about wine, except you have it at Christmas and on birthdays, and it's part of the dining room business, and sometimes, when it's really special, you get that fizzy stuff that comes in a bottle with gold paper on and it goes off with a bang. I like that. It's very partyish. Even if the bubbles do go up your nose.

Anyway, I wasn't getting very far with that so I went on to the French Revolution and how me and Mel knew all about it from the Scarlet Pimpernel. I thought it would please him that we knew so much and I wasn't just reading rubbish, like the "Bunty".

And I think it did and he was just beginning to listen and thaw out when I put my foot in it. I was telling them about the wigs when I said "They puff this powder on it to make it all white and then they backcomb it up into a sort of lump - you know, like David -" and the silence was so loud it rang in my ears.

Then Dad pushed his plate away. He shoved it so hard it went half way across the table and he said, "Don't mention that bastard to me." And for a minute he looked so angry, like he could kill David with his bare hands and enjoy every minute of it. I had never seen him look like that before and I never have since. Then he stood up and his chair scraped the floor really loudly and he said, "I'm sorry, I ..." but he didn't finish and he just took his drink and went into the study. He shut the door and he didn't come out.

Maggie picked up his plate and scraped it off into the bin. He hadn't eaten much.

"What's a bastard?" I knew it couldn't be anything good. Maggie sighed.

"A really bad person. Like David."

And that hurt me because it was wrong. I knew David and I knew how much he loved Julie. He never meant to hurt her. All that came from the railroading. Suddenly I felt angry, because I was being railroaded now. I was being railroaded into believing something I knew was not true. Something that I had seen, something wonderful, this huge love they had for each other was being turned into something bad, something dirty. It was a lie.

So I marched into Dad's study. He didn't want me there. He was in his armchair reading the paper with another glass of whisky by his side. He looked up at me. He wanted me to go away. I wasn't going to.

"Dad, David's not a bastard."

He put the paper down. "Yes, he is."

"No, he isn't, I know him and you don't. He's very kind and he really loves Julie and she loves him. And I don't care about the family name being high or low . I want them to be together because then she can be happy and this way I know she won't."

For a dreadful moment I thought he might cry.

His eyes went red and watery, but he looked away and said very quietly, " I know she won't, Sally, which is why I think he's a bastard."

"But you don't even know him!" That was a real wail. I

189

was Mum's daughter, all right. The wails came pouring out of you whether you wanted them to or not. He put his hand out to me and drew me over to him,

"Darling, I don't have to know him. What David has done is bad and very wrong. To have a serious love affair with another woman when your wife is expecting a child - and not tell either of them about the other one until it is too late and then get your girlfriend pregnant too, - I'm afraid that is being a bastard, Sally, whichever way you look at it."

I wasn't convinced. "He didn't mean to."

"He still did it, whether he meant to or not."

"Yes, but what happens if you fall in love - you know, swept off your feet - and you know it's all wrong, but you can't help it. " I was speaking from experience here. "You know, like in Mum's books! What then?"

He sighed at the mention of Mum's books. He didn't approve of them.

"Then maybe you just grow up and act like a man and ruin one life instead of three." He turned away. He'd had enough.

"Four actually, Dad, FOUR!" Suddenly, I was shouting, so angry that I could feel the pulse in my throat. I was crazy now, as crazy as Julie, full up with all the pain that was around me.

"Julie's baby is being killed right now! That seems pretty ruined to me!" I think I even stamped my foot.

I'd gone too far. I could see Maggie standing in the doorway. She had come to see what the shouting was all about.

Dad appealed to her."Take your sister away, Maggie. Make her calm down." He reached for his drink. He didn't look at me. He couldn't handle me. He couldn't handle Julie either. In times of trouble we didn't speak the same language.

Maggie took me out. She lead me back into the kitchen. Then she got me a glass of water. She and Dad always did that. If you were upset or going crazy, they gave you a glass of water. Perhaps they thought it would drown your feelings.

When I had drunk the water, Maggie put the empty glass on the draining board.

"What was that all about?" For once she actually sounded interested.

"David."

"Oh." You could tell she felt the same as Dad.

"He's not "Oh" and he's not a bastard either. He's the love of Julie's life."

"Yours too by the sound of it." She didn't sound angry. But I was. I had unravelled. I may have stamped my foot again.

"All right, he is the love of my life. So what? I haven't done anything wrong."

"I know. You haven't had the chance. Neither have I. " And she laughed. Her funny, dry sort of laugh that sounded as if she didn't do it very often. And I thought I would never understand Maggie. Not even if I lived to be as old as Aunty Katy. But I started to laugh too. Because what she said was true and I had told her my most awful secret and she didn't seem to mind. It was the most tremendous relief. Until I swallowed my spit and started choking and Dad came to see what was up. He looked disgusted with both of us.

"Shouldn't have thought there was much to laugh about tonight." He sounded angry again so we went into the sitting room and turned the telly on so he couldn't hear us. We sat on the sofa and laughed 'til we cried. We went crazy. We couldn't stop. It had all been too much for us. Even for Mags.

We lay on the sofa like we always did and pushed each other with our feet to stop the other one hogging all the room. Then we ate all the toffees from the "Quality Street" tin, the ones in the gold paper, and we watched "Bonanza". Ben Cartwright was having a terrible time with his sons. All of them. Adam, who was serious, Hoss, who was hideous and Little Joe, who was a dish. They were all a disaster really … just like us, only men. It was rather a comfort. But it didn't last because the toffees made me feel sick and I kept thinking of Julie, having her baby scraped out while we were on the sofa watching

191

"Bonanza".

When I went up to bed, I couldn't sleep. Mum wouldn't be asleep wherever she was. I knew that for sure.

It rained that night. For the first time in nearly five weeks. There was thunder and lightning, but it was still very hot and the air was thick and heavy. Then the rain began to fall, lightly at first - fine, gentle rain that barely wet the ground and then grew heavier until it became a downpour. I put my pillow on my desk and dragged it over to the window. Then I sat on it.

I opened the window and leaned out. There was a breeze now and the air was cooler. I watched the little puddles of rain form on the path and join up to make big ones as the rain continued to fall.

It fell all night long. I couldn't sleep, so I got Ted down for company and sat at the window and watched as the darkness faded into a grey and cloudy dawn and the garden became green again. Even our garden with it's sprinkler system had struggled in that heat. The grass had stayed okay, but the leaves on the outer bushes had begun to wither and go brown and some of Mum's plants had died. I watched the rain fall on the stones in the rockery and form tiny waterfalls that spilled over onto the flowers beneath.

I was very tired. But sleep was impossible. I felt bad about watching "Bonanza" and laughing with Mags, and I thought that somehow that if I stayed awake, if I kept watch with them, then Mum and Julie would be okay. Sounds daft, I know. But I knew they were awake too. I could feel it.

Dad was awake. I could hear him. He went downstairs while it was still dark and I didn't hear him come back up, so I supposed he was still down there. When it got light, I went downstairs. He was sitting in the kitchen drinking tea in his pyjamas, all unshaven with his hair on end.

He hadn't slept a wink either. He smiled when he saw me and ran his hand over his hair to smooth it down.

"Hello, poppet." He hadn't called me that for years. He poured me a cup of tea. "You couldn't sleep either?"

192

"Nope."

"You okay?"

I tried to explain. I didn't want to apologise because I wasn't sorry. "Dad, I ..." What could I say? That I was angry? Afraid? In love?

All of them were true, but there was nothing I could say that he would understand.

"I know, love, you were overwrought." I wasn't sure what that meant, but I nodded because he wanted to be friends. That was all that mattered.

So I drank my tea and read the comic strip on the back of his paper while he read the front page. We didn't talk because the news was very important to Dad. He didn't like interruptions.

Then he went upstairs to wash and shave and Maggie came down. She got our cereal out of the cupboard and poured the milk into a jug. She had slept all right. Nerves of steel, that girl. One giddy fit and she was back on the rails. It was going to take me a bit longer. Then Dad went to work and we got dressed and waited for Mum and Julie to come home.

CHAPTER 14

They didn't get back until after lunch. Maggie made us ham sandwiches. I didn't eat mine. It wasn't very nice and I kept jumping up every time I heard a car to see if it was them. So I gave up on it and went to watch at the window.

Mum had to help Julie out of the car. She was walking as if her knees had gone all wobbly. Mum put her straight to bed. She told us Julie needed to rest and not to disturb her, but I went up anyway to see if she was okay. She was lying in bed with the curtains drawn. She lay on her side with her legs drawn up to her stomach. Her skin looked sort of pasty and her eyes were all puffed up. She didn't have any make up on. I asked her if she was okay and she just sort of sighed and closed her eyes. She didn't say anything, so I went back downstairs.

For three days she stayed like that. Mum was all brisk and nurse-like and kept taking up tea and aspirins, but Julie wouldn't talk to anyone. Mum looked more and more worried. She started to make all the things Julie had always liked. To lure her back. Mashed potatoes and fried eggs, pancakes all light and golden, like only Mum could make them, rice pudding and raspberry jam. But it made no difference. She ate nothing. Nothing at all.

Maggie said to leave her be. That she needed time "to get over it". But I was frightened because she had so much to get over.

So every morning I used to go in to check on her. To see if she was okay. Well, still breathing actually, because you can die of a broken heart. It happens all the time in Mum's books. It's called "pining away." Victorian ladies did a lot of it. Julie

195

didn't speak to me when I asked her if she was okay, but sometimes she put out her hand and I held it.

After three days she got up. She had a bath and washed her hair and then she came downstairs. Mum made her an egg and she ate it. They talked a bit. I knew then that she would be okay. Mum spoke to Julie in her "let's be cheerful" voice and Dad kept asking her if she was okay which if anything was worse. What was she supposed to say? No?

They were all very nice to each other, but now they spoke in a kind of semaphore. Communication was kept to the minimum and feelings were not exchanged at all. Julie stopped wearing her nice things. She moped about the house in Mum's shirts that were too big for her and didn't show her bosoms. She didn't seem to be wearing earrings anymore.

I went back to the park with relief. At least Mel was normal and Tim and Rusty were great. We carried on where we had left off with the French Revolution. Mel and Tim knew I didn't want to talk about it. They respected my feelings. Friends do that. That's why they are better than family.

Then one day we were mucking about playing The Scarlet Pimpernel at Lady Grenville's Ball. We were lining up for the minuet when Tim said he wanted to do a new dance. He said it was called the waltz and it was okay because they did it in olden times too. But not in the French Revolution, said Mel. She put her foot down. No she said. They only did the minuet. She was a bit of a stickler with that sort of thing. But Tim just danced around her trying to catch her hand when she went past minuetting. He caught hold of her hand and pulled her over to him. Then he started whirling her round doing this waltz thing and I remembered where I had seen it before. It was the kind of dance Mum and Dad did at weddings. Tim said it was called the Viennese waltz and he kept whirling Mel around until she said she felt giddy and then he held her very tight against him. To stop her from falling over he said. He was holding her tight with both his arms around her so it looked like they were having a smooch. Rusty was running around, a bit bored I think, so I

196

threw a stick for him to run and fetch. Then suddenly Mel broke away from Tim. She went bright red and she looked really scared. She wouldn't dance with him after that. She wouldn't look at him either. She just said she was too tired and she went and sat under a tree with Rusty. Now that was peculiar because Mel could dance forever without getting puffed. So I went and joined her and I asked her what was up. But before she could tell me Tim came up and sat down beside us.

Then he said, "It's a scorcher today, all right ," and he took his shirt off. Then he leaned over to us and said "Why don't you take your shirts off? It's much too hot for all these clothes." I took no notice because I didn't want to take my shirt off. I said, "We don't undress in the park. It's bad manners." But Mel still looked a bit scared so I moved closer to her.

Then he started talking. He'd never talked like this before. The subjects seemed to run into each other and get all muddled up. He talked about the weather and the park and the other people and their dogs and then he started to talk about his mother. He never mentioned her before. He didn't seem to like her very much.

I didn't know what to say. Mel was starting to look quite panicky. In the end, she rolled over and pretended to be asleep. She turned her back on him which was very rude. Then she yawned. She was trying to make him go away, but he didn't take the hint. She looked pretty daft lying there like that with her knees bent up and her bum stuck out. Practically in his face, He didn't seem to mind.

He just stared at it and started to grin. I wasn't sure I liked this now. I closed my eyes too. Then he said, "Does your Dad ever spank you, Sally?"

Honestly. So I opened my eyes and said "Sometimes. Why?" And he laughed and said "On your bare bottom?" And he put his hand down his trousers and started to move it up and down.

I stood up then. "Come on, Mel. We're going home." And do you know what he said?

197

"Does he do it often?" in a pleading sort of voice and his hand was moving up and down faster and faster and his voice had gone all breathy.

Old Sleeping Beauty got up in a flash. I said to Mel, "Don't talk to him He's gone weird." We headed for the stream like bats out of hell. That's what Dad says when he means as fast as you can go. We sploshed across without bothering about the stepping stones. I was afraid he would follow us. But he didn't. Rusty did for a bit, but when we got to the edge of the park, he turned round and went back to his master. He was a very good dog.

I wanted to tell Mum all about it. But when I got home, she was bustling about the kitchen making a plum tart and looking grimmer than ever. I asked her what else could possibly have gone wrong. Then she told me that Julie had decided not to go back to Heggartys. It had something to do with not wanting to show her face, Mum said. Mum seemed to understand that. What she was less happy about was that Julie had rung her friend Annaliese. Annaliese lived in Austria with her parents when she wasn't skating with Julie. And she had asked Julie to come and stay with her in a place called Zell am See where her parents had a guesthouse. She said it was lovely there with the mountains and the lake, and Julie could stay for as long as she liked and help out in the guesthouse until it was time to go skating again and Julie had said yes.

Mum looked worried and a bit cross. They talked about it all through the Coronation chicken and the plum tart, so I never got the chance to tell her how Tim had suddenly gone all weird. They were too preoccupied with this now. Mum was dead against it, but Julie really wanted to go and she had an unexpected ally. Dad agreed with her. So Julie went into his study to make a trunk call to Annaliese in Austria and make the arrangements.

Mum looked at him and said it was too soon and she looked as if she might cry. Dad put his hand on hers and said very quietly that he knew that, but she must see that it was really

198

impossible for Julie to stay in Kenton now and risk bumping into David or Jeannie all the time.

He said that if she wanted to get away and stay with a friend, and we knew Annaliese and her parents, they had even stayed with us when they came over for the Wembley show and they were really decent people, why ever not, darling? he said, why ever not? Mum swallowed hard and said, "I don't want to let her go." And Dad said, "If you love her, Susan, let her go."

And we knew he must be very serious because he hardly ever called her Susan. Mum nodded her head and went all red and started stacking the plates in the sink. Then she began to cry and Dad put his arms round her, so Maggie and I left them to it. We never got round to Tim.

* * * * * *

And Julie went away. She packed her clothes in her big black suitcase and her make up in her little white vanity case and Dad took her to the airport. We didn't go with them, even though it was the holidays. Mum hugged Julie very tight and whispered that she must take care of herself. She had tears in her eyes. Julie hugged us all and said goodbye, but she was only going through the motions. In her heart she had already gone.

After they left, Maggie and I had one of those terrible games of Monopoly that go on for hours and nobody wins. Then Mum took her to see Sharon. While they were out, I wandered round the empty house. Past the hall where the window had been broken by Jeannie and her Mum and the study where Julie had learned that she could never see David again. The place was full of ghosts. I went upstairs.

Without thinking, I piled up my books and games and took them into Julie's room, like I always did when she went away. But it didn't feel right now. It still smelled of her hair lacquer so I opened the window. The window I used to watch her meeting David from every morning.

I wandered around and then decided to have a rummage in the dressing table to see if she had left anything behind. The top drawer was almost empty. I only found a bent hairpin, a cracked stub of eyebrow pencil and a pink lipstick that had gone gooey. Not much use really. And it was all dirty and dusty because she'd spilled her face powder I looked at myself in the mirror and wondered what I would look like when I grew up.

I opened the next drawer down. It was empty except for a small package. It wasn't very well wrapped up. It looked as if she had done it in a hurry.

On the outside she had written " For Madame Parker, my sister and my friend."

I opened it. Inside was a little box with her St Christopher medal on a gold chain. Mum and Dad had given it to her when she first went away skating. To keep her safe from harm. It had failed her. Now she wanted me to have it. I put it on, but I tucked it underneath my dress so no-one could see.

Then I went downstairs. I couldn't play in there anymore. Too much had happened.

CHAPTER 15

The day before we went to Paignton Mel and I went back to the park. We decided to risk it because Tim was never there that early. We didn't want to see Tim again because of him turning out to be weird. We were both going away. I was going to Paignton and after about a week, Mel was going to Wales, so we would be apart for three whole weeks. We were dreading it. Three whole weeks of undiluted family.

We had been going to Paignton since I was a baby. I loved it. We knew the people who ran the hotel, Mr and Mrs Lewis and their grown up daughter, Marion. The hotel was huge and had been grand. It was even called "The Grand" but its' grandness was running out. The paint was peeling on the window sills and the huge, cabbagey roses on the carpet faded a little more every year. I didn't care. I had been offered abroad, but I turned it down. I loved the big, empty ballroom with the little gilt chairs and the glassed in verandah where I used to read my comics when it rained. In Paignton there was a fairground and a model village and lovely little rock pools with brown shrimps in. And those peculiar things in shells that you put vinegar on and eat with a pin. There were rainbow coloured beach huts where you could shelter from the rain and hide the bucket and spade you didn't want to be caught dead carrying. We took the same one every year. It was painted pale blue and it was called "Balmoral".

Mum and Dad had talked about going abroad. To a place called Viareggio where a poet had died on the beach. I mean, I ask you! Maggie wanted to go abroad, all her friends did, she said, and it was lovely there because the sea was warm, which it never was in Paignton. But I said no. No, no, no. I wanted Paignton and walks along the cliff and ice cream and donkey rides on my beach, not dead people. I liked my sea cold, I said. And Dad and Maggie said that was because I never swam in it. Which was true. I don't trust the sea. Not to swim in. It's too big and too rough and it can storm up and sweep you away in no time at all. Gone. Vanished Forever. No, I like to do my swimming in a pool where people can see if you are drowning. So they said we could go to Paignton for one last time and then it would be abroad from then on.

Mel and I began our farewell tour of the park. We crossed the stepping stones and made for the trees and the field beyond. We had a lovely time playing and not fighting because you only realise how wonderful a friend is when you are about to spend three weeks with just your family. Then we got hungry. So we decided to get some chips. Sixpence worth. Each. A farewell feast.

We walked back through the trees to the stream. Tim stepped out from behind one of them. He must have been watching us. I couldn't see Rusty anywhere. He grabbed me by the shoulder, spun me round and pushed me up against a tree. Then he yanked my head back. He held me by my hair. I couldn't move. He was hurting me. His face came too close. I could feel his breath.

Then he kissed me. His lips were all wet and his teeth grated on mine. I tried to push him away, but he was too strong.

He forced my mouth open and stuck his tongue down my throat. I gagged. Everything was swimming round. I felt his hand between my legs pushing them apart. Mel was screaming. I kicked him - hard. He let go so suddenly I hit my head on the tree. It hurt.

His face was all covered in little silver flecks that shone like stars. I ran for it. Splashing across the stream, stumbling, falling, everything spinning in a crazy jumble of path and trees

202

and sky. I pulled myself up the slope and crashed straight into Mrs Braden. She was taking Secundo for his morning walk.

"Good God!" I held on to her like grim death. "What on earth?" I was smothered in dusty black wool. The fox dangled it's paws in my face. I screamed. Mrs Braden pulled me away from her and stared at me. Then her voice changed.

"You've cut yourself, you silly child." She touched the back of my head with her gloved hand. Then she pulled a tiny, white lace handkerchief from her coat pocket and dabbed at my head. By now Mel had caught up with us, panting and out of breath. "She didn't do it. He did. He tried to ..." And she pointed at Tim, who was running away through the trees. "Oh my God."Mrs Braden put her arms around me. Secundo started to bark. He didn't like having to share Mrs Braden.

" Oh do shut up, you stupid dog!!" Mel opened her eyes wide. Mrs Braden never shouted at Secundo. Only us.

"Come along, dear. We must get you home and cleaned up." Except she didn't take me to my home. She took me to Mel's. Because it was nearer hers, I suppose. She straightened her hat. It had got a bit skewiff in the crash. "Then we'll see about That Man." She sounded very stern. But her face was sweating and the powder was all clogged up in the lines around her mouth. She took us both by the hand and pulled old Secundo's lead so tight I thought she'd strangle him. Then she marched us back to Mel's, where Peggy dabbed at my head with some Dettol and called me "a poor wounded soldier." She wasn't much of a nurse. But Mrs Braden had been very kind in her own peculiar way. Which was rather a surprise.

Peggy made us sit down on the terrace. I couldn't eat anything because I still felt sick, but she made us a big jug of lemonade and said she'd see about lunch later. We sat on the steps and looked out across Mel's garden. I think we may have held hands because the morning had been a bit of an ordeal. Mel shivered. There was the first distant chill in the air. The roses had dropped their petals on the grass, like little silk shells. Summer was coming to an end. We would go away and when we came back, it would be autumn and there would be school.

I put my head on Mel's shoulder. It was boney and uncomfortable, but I wondered how I'd ever manage without her. She was my best friend, you see, even if she was a bit of a nit. And you could tell she was upset about what had happened because, although she didn't say much, she'd done the buttons on her cardi up wrong and she always did that when she was upset. She couldn't get them lined up right. "Mim", I always called her that when we felt extra specially close. It had been my name for her when we were babies. I couldn't say Melanie then. It's a bit of a mouthful for a toddler. She turned to look at me, her face all pale and anxious. She never went brown, Mel, not even in a heatwave. The sun didn't seem to work on her.

"Mim, shall we give up on this man business? For the time being? Because it's …it's just not …" She nodded in complete agreement.

"Yup. It's not worth it. I think we should leave it for later. " Which goes to show you how wise she could be. She sighed and put her skinny old arm round my shoulder. Then we looked at the garden together and drank our lemonade.

Peggy told Mum what Mrs Braden had told her. The police came back again and asked a lot of questions about Tim.

They began to patrol the whole area, including the park.

Not that it did us much good. We were forbidden on pain of death to go anywhere near the place. We never saw Tim or Rusty again.

Mum kept me under house arrest until we went away. She barely let me out of her sight. So it was just "Route 66" after that And Mum caught us in the car and all she said was, "Oh well, at least I know you're safe in the drive." That was a facer because it was strictly forbidden. She didn't seem to mind now. And she never told Dad.

* * * * *

So we went to Paignton and had our last holiday in England. And nearly every evening after dinner, which Maggie and I were now old enough to have with our parents in the hotel dining room, (instead of a lovely high tea on our own in the ballroom, which frankly was a lot more fun), Mags and I would walk to the end of the pier, past the theatre and amusement arcade, to the place where Julie used to take us when we were little. She had a pony tail then and no make up and she wore her cardigan over her shoulders to make her look older. She used to buy us candy floss which we weren't allowed, and we would share it and listen to the quiet rushing waves and look up at the stars. Julie knew what some of them were called. She told us their names. She loved them. She said they were "Tiny points of light in an ocean of darkness". Which showed you what a dreamer she was.

And Mags and I would look out across the sea and wonder where she was. Because although she was far away from us, she was still under the same sky, somewhere.

We didn't see Julie for a long time. We only saw her again when she came back to Wembley for the Christmas show.

And when she did come back, she was different. Older, not ours anymore. She talked a lot and laughed too loud in that stuck up, show biz way that seemed designed to shut you out rather than let you in. Maggie hated it. She listened to it for about two minutes and then she fled.

Julie wore too much make up now. Lots of green eyeshadow and orange lipstick and thick black lines around her eyes. Her hair was cut in a fringe. She said it was the "Cleopatra" look and all the rage, but when she wasn't talking or pulling faces, her face looked empty, like a mask. There was no-one behind it.

She brought a man with her. Her boyfriend, she said. He was called Frank. He was much older than she was and going

205

bald. I didn't like him much. Nor did she. You could tell. She never looked at him the way she had at David.

But she was different now and so were we. She had gone back to her lonely space on the ice where she could dance in a pool of light and no one could hurt her. Where she could live in a fairy tale and be safe.

And as for us - Mel and me - the summer had taught us that the grown up world was not safe. It only appeared to be. It was full of lies and rage and pain. And now that we had seen it, so were we.

FINIS

Lightning Source UK Ltd.
Milton Keynes UK
29 October 2010

162087UK00001B/150/P